"Are you okay?" Tess asked.

Mitch glanced to where her hand lay against his jacket and swallowed hard. "Sure. Shall we go?"

He reached across and grabbed the seat belt, drawing it across her abdomen, and his palm grazed her belly. She winced and he went to snatch his hand away, but suddenly she rested her own hand over his, holding him steady against her stomach.

"He's moving," she said quietly.

Mitch's chest tightened. "For real?"

She nodded and pressed his hand firmer. "Well, it's probably more like fluttering, but it feels...it feels... I guess it feels exactly like I'd hoped it would."

Mitch stilled, his palm burning where it lay against her rounded belly, and experienced an acute and riveting connection to the woman he'd loved and lost. So much had transpired between them, so much loss and anguish and despair. But in that moment, as her hand pressed firmly over his, all he felt was a surge of something so intense, so real, he could barely draw a breath.

And he knew he'd never really gotten over her.

Then he wondered what the hell he could do about it.

* * *

THE CULHANES OF CEDAR RIVER:
Family lost, family found

P9-CSF-059

Dear Reader,

Welcome back to Cedar River, South Dakota! And to my latest book for Harlequin Special Edition, *When You Least Expect It*. These characters came to me a long time ago and I'm delighted to tell their story at the beginning of my latest series for Harlequin Special Edition, The Culhanes of Cedar River.

Reunions are often fraught with memories—and for rancher Mitch Culhane and his ex-wife, Tess, remembering what broke them apart may just keep them that way. Mitch is a strong and stubborn man who is used to looking after everything and everyone, and not great at admitting there were things he couldn't fix—like his broken marriage to the only woman who ever had his heart. But now there's a baby on the way, a love to rekindle and an interfering though well-meaning family to keep them from giving up on one another.

I hope you enjoy Mitch and Tess's story and invite you back to South Dakota for my next book in The Culhanes of Cedar River series, coming December 2019. I love hearing from readers and can be contacted at helenlaceyauthor@gmail.com or via my website, www.helenlacey.com, or Facebook page to talk about horses, cowboys or how wonderful it is writing for Harlequin Special Edition. Happy reading!

Warmest wishes,

Helen Lacey

When You Least Expect It

Helen Lacey

HARLEQUIN® SPECIAL EDITION

ISBN-13: 978-1-335-57411-4

When You Least Expect It

Copyright © 2019 by Helen Lacey

This edition published by arrangement with Harlequin Books S.A.

For questions and comments about the quality of this book, please contact us at CustomerService@Harlequin.com.

Printed in U.S.A.

www.Harlequin.com

Helen Lacey grew up reading *Black Beauty* and *Little House on the Prairie*. These childhood classics inspired her to write her first book when she was seven, a story about a girl and her horse. She loves writing for Harlequin Special Edition, where she can create strong heroes with soft hearts and heroines with gumption who get their happily-ever-afters. For more about Helen, visit her website, helenlacey.com.

Books by Helen Lacey

Harlequin Special Edition

The Cedar River Cowboys

Three Reasons to Wed
Lucy & the Lieutenant
The Cowgirl's Forever Family
Married to the Mom-to-Be
The Rancher's Unexpected Family
A Kiss, a Dance & a Diamond
The Secret Son's Homecoming

The Fortunes of Texas: The Lost Fortunes

Her Secret Texas Valentine

The Fortunes of Texas

A Fortunes of Texas Christmas

The Prestons of Crystal Point

The CEO's Baby Surprise

Date with Destiny
Once Upon a Bride
Claiming His Brother's Baby

Visit the Author Profile page
at Harlequin.com for more titles.

For my wonderful friend, mentor
and fellow author Helen Bianchin.

One of the kindest, most gracious people I know.

Chapter One

Branding was backbreaking work, Mitch Culhane thought as he instructed two of his newest wranglers to head off a particularly bad-tempered steer who was trying in vain to escape the inevitable. But it needed to be done to ensure the cattle didn't end up getting lost or rustled before it was time to head to auction.

The animal wailed for a moment, and then, once it was released, raced around the corral and headed down the cattle chute. Mitch straightened, dropped the Triple C branding iron back into the embers and walked through the gate, grabbing the bandanna hanging from his back pocket to wipe his brow. He'd been up since dawn, planning to finish most of the branding before eight.

It was one of the coldest Octobers on record, but the clear blue South Dakota sky still had him thinking that he wouldn't want to be anywhere else in the world. He'd lived in Cedar River, a small town that sat in the shadow of the Black Hills, all of his life. About a forty-minute drive south of Rapid City, it had once been a busy mining town. Now, with its three thousand or so residents, it catered to tourists and commuters heading for the state line. A few of his neighbors had turned their places into dude ranches or farm-stay vacation destinations for curious city folk wanting to learn to milk cows or "get in touch with the land," or so he'd hear them say around town. But Mitch was determined to make the ranch viable and profitable, despite fluctuating beef prices and competition from import traders. The Triple C was his legacy, and he wasn't about to let the place go under... not on his watch.

He headed for the barn and made a path through the chickens pecking at the ground around the doors. His foreman, Wes Collins, was barking out orders to one of the ranch hands. He didn't interfere, since Wes was very capable of handling the crew. Instead, he headed for the far stall and leaned over the door. Dolly, the paint mare he'd bred and raised, was stomping around the stall impatiently, clearly in the late stages of labor. It wouldn't be long, he figured, maybe a couple of hours, before she gave birth to her first foal.

"You look worried."

Mitch swung around and spotted his younger sister, Ellie, striding toward him. He managed a half smile. "I'm fine," he assured her. "It's not the first foal to be born on the Triple C. Nor will it be the last."

"It's the first of the Alvarez foals," she reminded him, and raised her brows in her annoying way. "And I know you want everything to go off without a hitch."

"I want every foal to be born without complication— this one, too. You're the one who looks worried."

"Because we've got so much invested in this," she said, and sighed, swinging her brown ponytail. "And I still don't know why we had to go all the way to Arizona to get a stud. There are plenty of quality local stallions who could—"

"Because we needed something different," he said, harsher than usual. "You know that, Ellie. Local bloodlines aren't cutting it at auction anymore. And Alvarez has some of the best quarter horses in the country. We're lucky to get this deal. Don't blow it by being a hothead just because you don't like the guy."

"He called me a boy," she reminded Mitch indignantly, hands on her hips.

"Two years ago," he said, and grinned. "Let it go, okay. We both know that Dolly's foal will be a winner."

She nodded a little more agreeably. Whatever their difference of opinion when it came to the Alvarez deal, they both understood what the outcome meant for the ranch.

"I miss Rocket," Ellie said and sighed.

Mitch had been raising and training quality quarter horses for over a decade—but so were half a dozen other ranchers in the county. When his foundation stallion, Rocket, had died a few years earlier, he knew he had to make some changes so the ranch could stay solvent in the long term. The Alvarez deal was one part of that plan. And Dolly's foal, sired by Volcán, Ramon Alvarez's champion reining stallion, was the first of its progeny to be born outside of Arizona.

"I miss Rocket, too," he said and smiled. "But he's gone and we need this deal. We all worked hard to get Alvarez to agree to this, remember. Dolly's foal will be the start of something good for the ranch."

"Unless it's a filly and Alvarez gets to keep her," she reminded him.

Mitch shrugged. "That was part of the contract. Besides, we need a colt, you know that."

Ellie made a face, the way she used to as a child, and it made Mitch smile. In some ways he suspected he still treated her like a kid even though she was twenty-four. But old habits were hard to break. He'd raised her since she was eight and couldn't help his feelings sometimes. Even though he knew it irked her.

"You coming to the house for breakfast?" he asked.

"Not today," she replied. "I've got a mountain of reading to catch up on."

Ellie, who lived in the largest of the cottages behind the main house, was studying business and accounting as well as helping him on the ranch. She'd moved out of the ranch house at twenty-one, as part of her determination to be independent and away from his scrutiny, he figured. But she was still close enough for him to keep a watchful eye on his baby sister. A job he'd been doing for sixteen years, since their father, Billie-Jack Culhane had walked out on his family and left Mitch to raise all five of his siblings.

They chatted for a few more minutes, and then Mitch whistled for the dogs to follow and headed up to the house. Shanook, a tall wolfhound cross, was at his side immediately, and the smaller dog, Tubby, a border collie, wasn't far behind. He circumnavigated the house and strode through the back, leaving the dogs to laze on their beds by the entrance to the mudroom. Mrs. Bailey, the sixty-something housekeeper who had been on the ranch for over a decade, greeted him in the kitchen with a smile.

"Fried ham and eggs," she said. "Your favorite."

Mitch patted his belly and glanced at the plate sliding across the countertop. "You spoil me, Mrs. B."

Her crinkly face looked earnest. "Well, someone has to, the way you always look out for everyone else."

Mitch grabbed the plate and sat at the table. On the

surface, his day-to-day routine seemed uncomplicated and on an even tempo. But that was just the surface, the facade he clung to and showed the world. As the eldest of the Culhane siblings, he was the glue that had kept the family from being broken up and farmed out into social services and foster care. But the truth was that he lived his life very much alone.

And had done so since his wife had walked out on him four years earlier.

Tess...

With her warm brown eyes and long blond hair. Tess, with her tender touch and soft smile.

Just thinking about her made his insides ache, and he quickly pushed the memory of her from his thoughts. Tess was his past and was best left exactly there. Only... sometimes he hurt all over remembering all that they had been and everything they had lost.

Once he finished breakfast, Mitch helped Mrs. Bailey clean up before heading upstairs. He stalled at the top of the landing and glanced at the photographs on the wall. Six generations of Culhanes stared back at him. The old sepia snapshots of great-great-grandparents and next to them, his grandparents. He couldn't help thinking how much he missed them. He glanced sideways and spotted a picture of his parents in happier times. Before his mother had died. Before his father had become consumed by grief and lost himself in liquor and run out on his six children. Mitch had been granted guardianship of his five younger siblings once Billie-Jack signed over his parental rights, and he was happy to forget the old man even existed.

His gaze dropped to the more recent photos, and his feelings shifted to both melancholy and a good dose of pride. His siblings had matured into fine adults, all of them good people who lived rich and fulfilling lives. They were, he figured, his greatest achievement, and he loved each of them dearly and was grateful most of them still lived in town. Except for Jake, his brother closest in age by less than two years, who'd only been back to Cedar River a couple of times since joining the army when he was eighteen. Joss, who was a single dad, owned an auto repair shop in town, and Joss's twin, Hank was the chief of police. His youngest brother, Grant, had moved to Rapid City several years earlier and worked in IT, and Ellie lived on the ranch. They were a tight unit, bound together by blood and the echoes of the past.

Mitch kept walking and headed toward the master bedroom suite, which was spacious and offered a spectacular view of the ranch from its wide windows that opened onto a balcony. He entered the room and looked around. He hadn't slept in the room for years, preferring one of the smaller guest rooms down at the end of the hall, since Tess had walked out. Since Ellie had moved into one of the cottages and Grant had left, Mitch rattled around in the main house like a ghost. Not that he couldn't find company if he wanted it. A night out at the Loose Moose Tavern or the bar at the O'Sullivan Hotel would have been an easy option, and he had plenty of friends in town. But he was simply too busy for socializing. The ranch didn't run itself, and he had too much invested in the place to waste time on personal pursuits. Like dating. Or sex.

Well, except for that one time—five months, three weeks and four days ago.

With Tess.

He'd been in Sioux Falls at a conference and had bumped into his ex-wife at the hotel. At first it had been a surprise. And then awkward. And after that something else. And, somehow, one thing led to another, and after sharing coffee and some stilted conversation, they had ended up in his hotel room for a crazy few hours. It was one last fling, he figured. A way for the both of them to finally exorcize the other from their memories and move past their complicated history. He hadn't spoken to her since and didn't expect to ever again.

They were done. Over. He had to move on.

And he would...one day. Maybe he'd even get married again. He was only thirty-four. He still had time to find someone to share his life with.

I can forget her.

I have to.

Mitch took a long breath, rounding out his shoulders. He was about to leave the room when he spotted a small white car turning into the gate at the end of the long driveway. He wasn't expecting a visitor. Fridays were generally quiet on the ranch. The Triple C was several miles off the highway so a lost tourist was unlikely. He left the room and headed back down the stairs, figuring he find out who was intruding on his morning soon enough.

I must be out of my mind.

That's all Tess Fuller kept chanting to herself as she steered her car in the direction of the large ranch house that loomed ahead. The place was impressive and one of the biggest homes in the county. With its wide verandas and shuttered doors, the white two-story home sat against a backdrop of white fences and pastures that went as far as the eyes could see. Tess had been in awe of the place a decade ago, when she'd first begun dating Mitch, and then less than a year later when they'd married. And she loved the ranch house, with its spacious rooms, timber staircase and polished floorboards. Her memories of the five years she'd spent as Mitch's wife at the Triple C were suddenly acute as she drove up the long gravel driveway.

Her stomach knotted the closer she got to the house, and she fought every instinct she possessed—instinct that told her to turn around and forget the crazy idea she had that seeing Mitch was the next obvious step.

Then she briefly placed a hand on her belly.

The baby fluttered beneath her palm and Tess experienced a heady surge of emotion. After spending so much time believing she'd never be a mother, Tess felt a deep and abiding love for her unborn child. Of course she'd been shocked to discover that the few hours she'd spent between the sheets with her ex-husband so many months ago had left her pregnant, but she didn't have one iota of regret for the way things had turned out.

She pulled up to the left side of the circular driveway in front of the house and switched off the ignition. The house looked huge, an intimidating structure against a backdrop of green pastures and blue skies. It had been in the Culhane family for several generations.

Tess took a breath and pulled out the keys, grabbing her tote with her free hand. She looked toward the house, and within seconds the front door opened.

Mitch Culhane.

Six feet two inches of green-eyed, broad-shouldered swaggering handsomeness. The kind of man that women dreamed about. Perfect in every way. And her husband.

Ex-husband.

Tess made the mental correction immediately.

She had done the leaving. The divorcing. Mitch had wanted to work things out…to try to get past their differences. But on *his* terms. That's when his consideration had turned into arrogance and into a one-eyed belief that he was right…about *everything*. And a marriage with conditions wasn't something she was prepared to endure.

Four years later she had believed they were done. She lived in Sioux Falls; he lived in Cedar River. She had a job teaching high school English. Mitch had the Triple C Ranch. She hadn't expected to bump into him at the hotel in Sioux Falls. She hadn't been prepared for the way he made her feel. She hadn't believed they had anything left to say to each other. And in the end, it wasn't conversation that drew them back together for those few brief hours. It was pure and unadulterated attraction. Desire. Sex. And it had been good. Amazing. Heat and sweat and pleasure, and then reality had set in and she'd left after a brief goodbye, flippantly wishing him a happy life, trying to hide the fact she was suddenly desperate to remain in his arms for the rest of eternity. Because his arms weren't hers to long for anymore. They were a memory. Their marriage was over and they both needed to move on. And she had intended to do exactly that.

Except for one tiny hiccup—now she was pregnant.

She watched him stride across the wide veranda, saw him come to a halt at the top step and place his hands on his lean hips. In worn jeans and a regulation chambray shirt, sheepskin-lined jacket, a bandanna hanging out of one pocket and his Stetson at a rakish angle, he looked like the postcard image of a Midwestern cowboy. And utterly gorgeous. Her insides did a silly flip-flop and she cursed herself for being so predictable. She'd known it wasn't going to be easy facing him again, particularly in light of her situation, but it had to be done. Mitch had every right to know he was going to be a father. Other than that, Tess didn't have any real expectations. She knew him, knew he was honorable to the core and certainly would step up and *be* a father, even if it were only part-time. She didn't anticipate any real problems arising.

The dogs came around the veranda and he immediately called them to heel. They obeyed instantly, sitting on their haunches, watching Mitch's movements with keen and loyal eyes.

She got out of the car, clutched her tote against her belly and closed the door. He was down the steps in three seconds flat, his handsome face furrowing into a tight frown more apparent with each step he took.

When he was on the other side of her car, he greeted her suspiciously. "Tess."

She swallowed hard. He didn't look pleased to see her. In fact, he looked downright annoyed. She should have expected it. Should have known he wouldn't want her back on the ranch, intruding in his life. For all she knew he could have moved on. There could well be a new mistress on the Triple C. It wasn't something that bore thinking about. And she couldn't explain why she ached inside just considering the possibility.

"Hello, Mitch."

He tipped his hat back a little and glared at her. "What are you doing here?"

"I need to talk to you."

"What about?"

Tess went to take a step, realizing he'd figure out exactly why she was at the ranch the moment she moved from around the vehicle. And then she decided there was little point in avoiding the inevitable. She took a deep breath and walked around the hood, her long-sleeved smock top and unbuttoned jacket doing little to disguise her protruding belly.

He stared incredulously, jaw adrift, eyes narrowing with a kind of gathering disbelief. And he hadn't moved an inch, she realized, as the seconds ticked by. He simply continued to stare, his attention moving downward and lingering on her abdomen for a moment before returning to meet her eyes.

"I'm pregnant," she said quietly, inhaling a steadying breath.

"Yes, I can see that."

Tess took a step closer. "It's your baby."

She watched, fascinated, as his throat convulsed as he swallowed hard. He was in shock, but in typical Mitch fashion, he would act as though he was in complete control. A virtue. And a flaw.

Because his one weakness was *not* being able to show weakness.

He blinked a couple of times, as though digesting her words, and then shook his head. "What did you say?"

Tess pushed back her shoulders. "I said, the baby is yours, Mitch. That afternoon at the hotel in Sioux Falls when we—"

He waved a hand, cutting her off. "Yeah, I know how babies are made, Tess."

Of course he did. They'd had plenty of practice, after all. This was the fifth baby they'd made together. Only, tragically, the last four of her pregnancies had all ended in miscarriage.

But not this time.

This time she was going to carry her child to full term and deliver a robust and healthy baby. She was sure of it. And since her doctor was also confident she would sustain the pregnancy, Tess had no intention of spending the next few months afraid she would lose her child. This time she *felt* different.

"I thought you should know," she said quietly. "So, I guess I'll head off and—"

"Don't be ridiculous," he said, cutting her off again. "Come inside and we'll talk."

He turned on his heels and jogged up the porch steps, not waiting for a reply, but she noted that he did hold the door for her. Tess rolled her eyes, and then followed. She should have known what to expect when she drove out here. The dogs greeted her with their tails wagging, and she patted them both enthusiastically before she passed Mitch by the door, ignoring the way her senses were suddenly on red alert around him. He closed the screen once she'd crossed the threshold and ushered her into the front living room.

Nothing much had changed, she thought as she entered the room. Except for the fact that their wedding portrait no longer hung on the wall near the fireplace. A watercolor hung there now, something abstract and impersonal that was the complete antithesis of the intimate photograph that had graced the spot for the entirety of their marriage. Of course, she hadn't expected that he would keep the portrait up once they were divorced.

"Is Mrs. Bailey still—"

"Yes," he replied gruffly. "She's in the kitchen. Do you want something? Coffee? Tea, maybe? I could ask her to—"

"No," she said, and waved a hand. "I'm fine. I only wondered if she was still here, that's all." Tess had always liked Mrs. Bailey. The older woman had been a friend and confidante during the years she'd lived at the ranch.

"Does your sister know you're in town?" he asked flatly.

Tess nodded. "I'm staying with her while I'm here."

"At David's?"

She nodded again. David McCall, a widower, was Mitch's cousin. Her stepsister, Annie, worked for David as nanny to his two children. Annie lived at David's ranch, which was about a twenty-minute drive from the Triple C.

"I only arrived this morning and came straight here. I called Annie last night and asked if I could stay for a few days," she said, and shrugged a little. "And I didn't elaborate. I just asked her to ask David not to say anything about me being in town to you or anyone else."

"So, who knows you're pregnant?"

"You," she replied. "But it's not like I can hide the fact from the world. Nor do I want to. I'm not unhappy about the baby, Mitch. In fact, I'm happier than I've ever been."

"Except for the part about me being the father, right?"

She stilled, and a familiar hurt, as raw and fresh as it had been four years earlier, wound its way through her blood. They'd said a lot of hurtful things to one another in the end. Words that would never be forgotten and could never be taken back.

"I'm not unhappy about that," she said quietly. "Despite…despite everything."

He laughed humorlessly. "Despite saying the last thing you wanted was to have a child with me."

Tess's back straightened as memories banged around in her head. "We both said things that day…things that we probably now regret."

"I don't," he said flatly. "I meant what I said. And if we could go back for a do-over, I'd say the same thing and feel the same way."

Tess's blood stilled in her veins. Four years later and he still didn't understand.

She clutched her tote to her hips, met his gaze and took a long breath. "Then I guess we have nothing else to say to one another."

His brows rose. "Oh, I think there's plenty to say, Tess. And I have to ask the obvious question—are you sure?"

She swallowed hard, knowing exactly what he meant. "Am I sure the baby is yours? Yes," she said quietly. "I'm positive."

"Because?"

"You're the only man I've been with in the last six months."

He gave her a vague nod and then moved around the room, dropping onto the couch. He rested his elbows on his knees and ran a weary hand through his hair. "So… what are your plans?"

"To have a healthy baby."

He didn't move an inch. "And where do I fit in?"

"That's your choice, Mitch. I know you probably have mixed feelings about it, considering our history. But I want you to know that I don't expect anything from you."

His eyes glittered brilliantly, and she could feel the building tension emanating from him, creating a kind of uneasy energy in the room. Once, she'd been able to read him like a book. But now, with so much time and recrimination between them, Tess felt as though she were almost looking at a stranger.

"That's very generous of you," he said quietly. Too quietly. And Tess wasn't fooled. He was mad. "You seem to have it all figured out."

Tess took a step back. "You're angry?"

"Perceptive," he said, and shot to his feet. "But not quite accurate. I'm…confused."

"By what?"

"We used a condom."

Okay. She hadn't considered the possibility that he would question the baby's paternity.

"I guess it must have broken." She shrugged her shoulders. "Sometimes that happens."

"So I have heard," he said quietly. "But you must know that the last thing I would want is to risk getting you pregnant again."

As he said the words, Mitch knew they would hurt her. But damnit, he was hurting, too. He couldn't push down the heavy ache rising up in his chest that quickly grabbed around his ribs like a vice and made breathing steadily almost impossible.

She was staring at him, her eyes shining. Of course she knew that he wouldn't have *wanted* to get her pregnant. He'd said as much right before she walked out all those years ago. But he was right to say it. Right to remind her.

"Of course I know that," she said stiffly, clearly reading his mind. "You made your opinion on the matter abundantly clear four years ago."

No more babies.

That's what he'd said. After her fourth and final miscarriage he told her they were done trying to have a family, and he'd watched helplessly as his grief-stricken wife had wept with sadness and despair.

And then he witnessed her resentment setting in.

But his reaction and feelings were valid. Every time she lost a child he had to watch her lose a little of herself, as well. Her anguish was inconsolable. Her despair heart wrenching and excruciating to observe. He'd tried to comfort her, but she withdrew more with each loss. In the end, he couldn't bear seeing her in so much pain. So, he did what he felt he had to do to protect her. He changed the rules, made it clear that he had no intention of fathering any more children with her.

They were done trying to have a baby.

At first, her reaction had been one of disbelief and

anger. Then she had tried to seduce and cajole and convince him it was worth the risk. But Mitch wouldn't budge, knowing she was far too emotional to see the reality for what it was. *Their reality.* They would have one another, and that would need to be enough.

Only, it hadn't been enough for Tess.

Days later she moved out and left town, and soon after she filed for divorce.

Looking at her now, so close, he realized how much he'd missed her…and yet, he could feel the divide between them growing with each passing second. His gaze dropped to her belly. *His child.* Could it really be true? Had that crazy and impulsive afternoon resulted in a baby? He knew that Tess wouldn't lie to him. If she said the baby was his, then he believed her. He knew it would be far less complicated and much easier for her if her baby *wasn't* his. She wouldn't have had to return to Cedar River. She could have continued on with her life, and they might never have seen one another again.

But that wasn't to be.

He experienced a mix of emotions. Fear was at the top of the list. She'd never gotten as far along in a pregnancy…and if she lost this child, Mitch suspected she might never recover. But she looked well… In fact, she was glowing. And he had a whole bunch of questions he wanted answered.

Chapter Two

Mitch took a long breath, calming the uneasiness simmering in his gut. "How…how is everything?" he asked quietly.

Her hand immediately rested on her middle. "Good. The baby is perfectly healthy and right on schedule. And I feel fine. My doctor thinks I'll—"

"Why are you only telling me now, Tess?" he demanded, sounding sharper than he liked, but unable to contain his confusion and growing irritation.

"I needed to be sure," she said, and shrugged again. "You know I've never been able to get past sixteen weeks. But this time…this time I did, and once my doctor assured me everything would be fine, that's when I knew I needed to tell you. If I'd miscarried early, then I wouldn't want you to go through that all over again. I didn't see the point."

Mitch couldn't believe what he was hearing. "So, you get to make all the decisions, correct?"

"I only wanted to—"

"Control me and my rights as this child's father?"

"I was trying to make things easier for us both," she implored. "And besides, we didn't exactly make any promises to one another that afternoon in Sioux Falls. It was just—"

"Sex?" he shot back. "Yes, I got that message loud and clear when you hightailed it from my room."

Memories of that afternoon bombarded his thoughts. Tess looking shocked to see him in the hotel foyer. Their first uncomfortable words. An awkward offer to have coffee. And then, things shifted on some invisible axis and suddenly a rekindled desire took control. They got to his room in record speed and made love like they had never been apart, with a kind of frenzied need that left them both exhausted and sated. What he'd expected afterward, Mitch wasn't sure. But it certainly wasn't Tess's quick and clearly uncomfortable exit.

"I thought it was best if I left without a postmortem," she said, slicing through his thoughts. "And neither of us could have known at the time that the contraception had failed."

She was right. But that wasn't the point. "You should have told me the moment you discovered you were pregnant."

Her chin angled higher. "I made my decision because I didn't want things to get too complicated."

"Too little, too late,'" he said, and glanced at her belly. "Don't you think?"

She moved around the sofa, arms crossed, her chin tilted at a determined angle. "I'm not here to argue with you, Mitch. I came to tell you about the baby. If you want to be a part of his life, then fine. If not, that's fine, too."

Mitch's expression narrowed. "His life?"

She smiled a little. "I think it's a boy."

Mitch's gut tightened. "You think? Have you had the test done?"

She shook her head. "I just feel like it's a boy. My doctor recommended I have the test done, you know, because of my history. But I thought we should find out together." She hesitated. "If...if you want to, that is."

A baby. They were having a baby. A thousand feelings coursed through his blood and across his skin before finally settling beneath his rib cage. Regret. Anticipation. Rage. Despair. Fear. Things he'd felt before. Things he'd never wanted to feel again. And something else. Joy. Happiness. Things he was terrified of feeling because they were always taken away.

"Yes...of course," he said quietly, pushing back the emotion in his voice and saw that, despite the way things were between them, she looked infuriatingly calm. And, of course, she *was* calm. She'd had months to prepare herself. Months to get used to the fact that she was going to be a parent.

Not ten minutes.

Mitch stalked across the room, heading for the fireplace. He placed his hands on the mantel and took a few long breaths, trying to find clarity in his thoughts. Tess was in his living room. Tess was having his baby. It seemed impossible and yet achingly real.

"What are your plans now?" he asked again as he turned to face her.

She sighed and pushed back her shoulders. "To stay. I plan on having the baby in Cedar River. I like this town. My sister is here, and I like the idea of being close to family. And you're here."

"Which means?" he asked.

"Which means I want our baby to have two parents.

I've resigned from my job in Sioux Falls and will stay with Annie until I find a place of my own. I'll go back to work part-time once the baby comes."

He crossed his arms. "You don't need to stay with your sister," he said flatly, thinking fast, and above the white noise screeching through his ears. "You can move back in here."

Her eyes became as wide as saucers. "I didn't come here so we could pick up where we left off, Mitch. Or to interrupt your life. For all I know you could be seeing someone and I—"

"I'm not seeing anyone," he said quickly. "Are you?"

She touched her belly again. "No. I'm single and plan on staying that way. I also plan on raising this child with the proviso that you can have as much or as little input as you would like."

"This child is a Culhane," he reminded her. "And he *or* she has a birthright. Which is this ranch *and* my name. Do you really think for one minute that I would deny my child either of those things?"

Her cheeks instantly blotched with color. "For someone who doesn't want children, you're sounding very—"

"I have never said I didn't want children," Mitch said, cutting her off as rage and helplessness filled his chest. "I said I didn't intend to get you pregnant again."

"If I remember correctly, you threatened to have a vasectomy!"

And there it was. The real reason she had left. Her words were loud and accusatory and the raw truth. He *had* said he would have the procedure done, to do his part to prevent the failed pregnancies. But instead of ending her determination to have a baby, it had ended their marriage. Mitch knew she believed his intention to take children off the table as an act of betrayal. She was wrong.

Tess was the one who betrayed their marriage by acting as though they weren't strong enough to survive without children to bind them together.

"You know why," he said, and propped his hands on his hips. "You were being completely unreasonable."

"Because I wanted to have a baby?"

"Because you put that want above everything else," he shot back. "Regardless of what that did to our relationship."

She tilted her chin in that defiant, annoyed way he was used to. Nothing had changed between them. The feelings were still there. The resentment that had driven them apart. The irony of the situation wasn't lost on Mitch. Their marriage had ended because he'd refused to try again. And now, here she was, in his living room, back in his life, because of one crazy afternoon. All because he couldn't control his damned libido when it came to his wife. *Ex-wife*, he corrected.

But, heaven help him, she was so beautiful. And pregnancy had only amplified her loveliness. Her skin was luminescent, her cheeks tinted with color and even though her brown eyes were regarding him with outrage, he couldn't help the way his blood heated simply by being in the same room.

And it had been like that from the beginning.

He was twenty-four when they met, she was twenty-one and in her first year teaching at the local high school. Born and raised in Rapid City, she'd taken the job in Cedar River when her parents moved to Wyoming. Mitch had been called to the school to discuss his younger brother Grant's failing grades. Tess had been standing in the classroom, her attention focused on wiping down the whiteboard. And he was a goner. Lust at first sight had been replaced quickly by a deep and abiding love within weeks of their first date. And ten months after they met, they married in a lovely ceremony with their families and friends present. She moved to the ranch, continued to teach part-time at a local school, and also took over the reins of running the house and helping with Ellie and Grant, who still lived at home. With Tess at his side, Mitch felt as though he finally had someone who could share the responsibility of being head of the Culhane family.

But five years and four failed pregnancies later, and they were over.

"Tess!"

Ellie's high-pitched shriek cut through his thoughts. Mitch snapped his head around and spotted his sister in the doorway, eyes as wide as saucers.

"Hello, Ellie," Tess said gently.

His sister was in the room in seconds and quickly hauled Tess into a hug. Which was when she pulled back and stared down at his ex-wife's protruding belly. "Oh, my goodness…you're pregnant?"

Tess nodded and glanced toward Mitch. "Yes."

"Congratulations," Ellie said with genuine warmth. "I know what this must mean to you. I didn't realize you'd gotten married again. Last time I bumped into Annie she didn't say anything."

"I'm not married," Tess said quietly.

"Oh, then who…" Ellie was a smart young woman, and it took barely a moment for her to look at Mitch and jerk a thumb in his direction. "Are you…is the baby…? Have I missed something here? Are you guys back together and—"

"No!" Tess said quickly.

Mitch noticed the way Ellie winced and he offered his sister an assuring smile. "What Tess means, is that, yes, we *are* having a baby. And we're trying to work out what that means."

Ellie didn't look altogether happy. "I don't understand…"

"Your brother and I bumped into one another at a conference in Sioux Falls six months ago," Tess said evenly. "We slept together and now I'm pregnant. That's the whole story."

Ellie pressed a hand to her forehead in the kind of dramatic expression he expected. His little sister was never one to hold back her feelings. "But shouldn't you guys get back together again or something? I mean, you're having a baby together. This is a *huge* deal."

"Ellie," Mitch said quietly. "Please don't interfere."

She scowled. "Are you serious? *You're* saying that to *me*? You constantly interfere in my life."

Mitch pushed back his temper. He adored Ellie, but she expressed every emotion without a filter, while he was exactly the opposite.

"It's complicated," Tess said, and Mitch saw the flicker of unity in her eyes. For now, at least, they were on the same side. "Your brother and I will work this out. For the moment, I'm going to stay in Cedar River and have the baby. My old friend Lucy is a doctor at the local hospital, so she's going to make sure I see an obstetrician and get prepared for the birth."

Mitch listened as she talked and admired the way she had quickly defused Ellie's outrage. Tess knew his sister well, and her softly spoken words had an instant effect. By the time she finished speaking, Ellie was nodding and talking about planning a baby shower.

"In a month or two," Tess assured her. "Okay? It's still too soon. And I know Annie will want to help with the plans. You can talk with her about the arrangements. But please wait until I have had a chance to talk to her first."

Ellie nodded and grinned. "Sure. I promise. So, tell me everything," she said, and chuckled. "You two hooked up at a hotel?"

He was relieved when Tess replied. "I was visiting a friend who works there, and your brother was at a conference and...things happened."

"It sounds romantic," Ellie said, and raised her brows. "And like fate. I mean, what were the chances of you both being there at the exact same time?"

"Coincidence," Tess replied.

Heat crawled up Mitch's neck. He certainly didn't want to have a discussion with his little sister about his relationship with Tess, because he had no idea what the status of their relationship was. Exes, certainly. Friends, definitely not. There was too much old baggage for them to ever be friends. And a few hours getting it on in a hotel room wasn't enough to make them real lovers.

He looked at Tess. She was tired but trying to hide the fact.

The reality of the situation hit him with the force of a freight train. It didn't matter that their marriage was over or that they had said countless regretful things to each other. The past suddenly seemed like a lifetime ago. It was the future that mattered. The future was all he could control.

They had a baby coming.

Which changed everything.

Yeah...things were definitely going to change.

Exhaustion seeped through Tess from head to toe. It had been a long and anxious drive, and being at the ranch and seeing Mitch again had depleted all her energy. She wanted to crawl into bed, pull up the covers and sleep like a hibernating bear for as long as possible.

Not even Ellie's sudden enthusiasm for a baby shower and baby shopping increased her energy levels. She sighed and dropped her shoulders. Glancing toward Mitch, she saw his gaze narrow and realized he knew exactly what she was feeling.

"Ellie," he said, and touched his sister's elbow. "Tess and I need to talk for a while. How about you go and ask Mrs. Bailey to make coffee and we'll be in the kitchen soon."

The younger woman frowned and then nodded. "Sure, but don't be long. We've got so much catching up to do."

Once Ellie left the room, Tess raised her brows. "She is a whirlwind."

He grinned fractionally. "Always was. Always will be."

"We still keep in touch occasionally," she admitted. "I wasn't sure if you knew that."

"I suspected," he replied, and fiddled with a couple of ornaments on the mantel. "I saw the birthday card you sent her last year and I know your handwriting."

Tess shrugged lightly. "I didn't mean to overstep. I know I should have—"

"You've known Ellie since she was a teenager. You helped raise her. It makes sense that you would want to maintain a connection."

Guilt pressed between her shoulders. "She probably didn't tell you because she didn't want to feel as though she betrayed—"

"I'm not angry, Tess," he said quietly, cutting her off. "I'm glad you stayed connected to Ellie. It will make things easier."

Tess frowned. "What things?"

"You and me things," he replied calmly, turning back around to face her. "Raising our child together."

Tess stilled and her breath caught in her throat. "We're not really doing that. Yes, *we* will be raising our child... but not together."

He came around the sofa, watching her, the burning intensity in his gaze searing through to the blood in her bones. Then he spoke. "I want shared custody."

"But I—"

"Fifty-fifty," he said. "Nothing less."

Tess felt as though her feet were suddenly stuck in cement. This wasn't what she had expected. Parental rights, certainly, but not a shared-custody arrangement. She inhaled heavily. "It's not up for negotiation."

"Exactly," he said.

"You're hardly in a position to look after a baby even in a shared capacity, Mitch, since running the ranch takes all of your time."

"I'll make time for my child," he assured her, his voice firm and clearly unassuageable.

His child.

Right. The line had been drawn. Tess met his gaze evenly. God, he was ridiculously handsome. She could barely look at him without thinking about that crazy afternoon just a few short months ago. In a moment of madness she had succumbed to every dormant fantasy she harbored about him. Chemistry like that didn't just fade, particularly considering how abruptly their marriage had ended. It had simply lain in wait, waiting to be fanned back into life. Waiting for their paths to cross so they could rekindle the incredible connection they had always had. Mitch hadn't been her first lover, but he was the only one who had mattered. He was the only man she had ever loved.

He was also the only man who had ever broken her heart.

The moment he'd told her he intended to have a vasectomy, Tess had shut down. It was the ultimate betrayal. His way of denying her what she so desperately wanted. His way of controlling her because Mitch Culhane had to control everything and everybody. And while she understood why he was like that, because he'd been forced to step up at eighteen and take care of his family, Tess had no intention of allowing Mitch to control *her*. She was her own woman, independent and quite capable of deciding what she wanted and needed. And having a child was on the top of her list.

"I didn't come here to argue about this, Mitch," she said, firmer this time. "I'll let you see as much of the baby as you want, but he or she will live with me."

"Perhaps I didn't make myself clear, Tess," he said quietly. "I have no intention of being a part-time father. And this isn't just your decision. It's *our* child, remember? That is what you came all this way to tell me, isn't it?"

She took a breath and turned, walking to the window, looking out at the fields, her arms crossed over her chest. She wasn't going to be cornered. She'd made her plans—come to Cedar River and tell Mitch about the baby, find a house close to her sister and deliver her child at the local hospital. Get a job. Live her life. Raise their child to know he or she had two loving and committed parents.

"Are you really going to be hardheaded about this?" she demanded. "And start making demands about custody even before the baby is born?"

"You don't get to make all the rules, Tess. I have as much at stake in this as you do, even if you're too selfish to see it."

"Selfish?" she shot back, outraged. "Are you kidding?

You're the one who needs to control everyone. I came here to tell you about the baby and—"

"You came here on your terms and in your own time," he replied so quietly she had to step closer to catch his words. "You're *six months* pregnant, Tess, and yet you're only telling me about this now. Why? Because you wanted to keep me in my place?"

Tess held her chin up. "That wasn't my intention. I was really struggling with all this myself, Mitch, okay? And arguing isn't helping."

"I agree," he said, and offered a tense smile. "In fact, we should probably head to the kitchen before Ellie sends out a search party."

Tess knew he was trying to defuse her *and* the situation. But the last thing she wanted was a full-blown argument about the way things were between them with both Ellie and Mrs. Bailey in the house. So, she agreed and walked toward the door, conscious of how close they were as she passed him. She noticed he had grime on his cheek and his jeans were dusty—he had clearly been working before she'd arrived.

By the time she reached the kitchen, Mrs. Bailey was already walking toward her, arms outstretched. The older woman was as warm and welcoming as she remembered, and Tess swallowed back the burn in her throat. The kitchen, with its wide cedar countertops and shaker-style cabinets, was so familiar that she took a second to look around. Memories assailed her—learning how to bake with Mrs. Bailey, cooking up a stack of pancakes late at night with Mitch, sitting at the table with a cup of hot chocolate on a late winter's afternoon and staring out at the sprawling ranch through the window. Long-ago memories, tucked away because they were filled with regret and bitterness and loss.

"How wonderful to see you," Mrs. Bailey said, and stood back, her gaze making a beeline for Tess's abdomen. Resting her gentle palm there for a moment. "And a baby is coming, what a lovely blessing."

Tess's eyes burned. Yes, her child was a blessing. And everyone in the room knew the road she had traveled to get to where she was, through loss and disappointment and bone-aching grief.

She turned a little and looked at Mitch. His green eyes burned into hers, stoking the fires of awareness that had been between them from the first time they'd met. Mitch had arrived at her classroom to discuss his younger brother's failing English grade, and she'd been knocked breathless. In jeans and chambray, boots and buckled belt, his hat in his hands, Tess had never met a more attractive man in her life. The slick suit-and-tie city boys she'd dated in the past quickly became a dim memory. She'd done her best to concentrate on the meeting, but a part of her kind of floated through the moment, and on reflection, realized she'd observed him as though she'd never met a handsome man before in her life. But she was instantly smitten by his rancher's swagger and the way he fitted out his blue jeans.

Ten years later, Tess *still* wasn't immune to his good looks and the undeniable chemistry they shared. Case in point, jumping into bed with him in Sioux Falls.

In some vague, faraway place, she heard Mrs. Bailey mention something about having made coffee for Mitch and tea for the rest of them and how she'd put out her famous walnut-and-date loaf. And all the while, Tess kept her gaze connected with his. She placed a hand on her belly and watched as he observed the movement, their connection amplifying as the seconds ticked by.

We're having a baby...

It had never felt more real to her than it did in that moment, and a profound sense of joy washed over her. And trepidation. And fear. Because she couldn't deny that they were now joined together for the remainder of their lives. Their child would be an undeniable connection. A catalyst for change. Not knowing what that looked like scared Tess to pieces.

"So, what's going to happen?"

It was Ellie's voice cutting through the silence. Her former sister-in-law was eyeing them curiously, clearly eager to know what they had planned for the future. Tess managed a small smile and was about to reply when Mitch spoke.

"Isn't it obvious?" He took a few steps toward her, unexpectedly grasping her hand.

"Obvious?" Tess echoed, trying to pull her fingers free of his touch. Trying not to react to the feel of his skin against hers. "What's obvious?"

His next words shocked her to the core.

"We'll have to get married."

Chapter Three

Mitch knew he had taken a huge chance making the unofficial announcement in front of his sister and house-keeper, but he also knew he needed every edge he could get.

Tess was mad at him. In fact, she was furious. But he was angry, too. She had no right to keep her pregnancy from him for so long. And she had no right to offer the crumbs of being "involved." He wanted to be a full-time father…and he would do a damned better job than his own ever had.

He watched her face flush, a sign of the emotion churning within her—but he wasn't going to be deterred. They would get married again, be a whole family for their child. It was the only possible course of action. Mitch took her hand in his and gently pulled her closer.

"That's so wonderful," Ellie said, clearly delighted. "I can't wait. When's the wedding?"

"Soon," Mitch assured his excited sister.

Tess was tense beside him, but he knew her well enough to realize she wouldn't make a scene in front of his sister or Mrs. B. He also knew he'd be in for one hell of a telling-off when they were finally alone.

"Boss?"

Mitch turned his head toward the door that led to the mudroom. Wes stood by the door, hat in his hand.

"Yes?" Mitch asked.

"Dolly's in some trouble."

Mitch released Tess's hand. "I'll be back soon," he said quietly, "so we can talk some more."

He excused himself and strode across the room, grabbing the spare Stetson he kept on the hook by the back door. He followed the other man through the door and out of the mudroom, and headed for the stables. Sure enough, Dolly *was* in trouble. Her foal was breech, and quickly Mitch called the vet hospital in town. He had handled breech births before, but wasn't about to take any risks with Dolly's safety. He soothed the agitated mare as best he could and waited for the vet to arrive.

Ryan Holt had taken over old Doc O'Rourke's practice a year earlier. Mitch had confidence in the younger man's skill, and two hours later, the mare gave birth to a healthy colt. It was past twelve o'clock by the time the colt was on his feet and suckling his mother.

In between helping to deliver the foal, he fielded calls and texts from three of his brothers. Ellie, it seemed, had taken it upon herself to announce the news of Tess's pregnancy to the family. He replied as casually as he could, saying Tess was moving back to Cedar River and he'd speak to them all soon to explain the situation in more detail.

He was placing hay in a net by the door when he spotted Tess walking toward him. Ellie had been back and forth all morning, checking on the foal, then doing a happy dance when the colt arrived because it meant they would be keeping him, instead of sending the foal to the Alvarez ranch in Arizona. There were two more foals due in the next couple of months and another round of insemination planned for three of his best brood mares. It was a busy time at the ranch. But not so busy that Mitch could ignore what was most important.

Tess.

She'd had remained in the house and Mitch was surprised she hadn't embraced the opportunity to take off and put some space between them. Instead, she'd stayed. Now Mitch figured they were about to pick up the conversation that had ended in the kitchen.

"Hey," he said, and continued to stuff hay in the net, ignoring the way his stomach twitched as she walked toward him, her hips swaying, looking so effortlessly beautiful he was struck by an inexplicable surge of attraction for her.

"We need to talk," she said flatly, hands on hips, chest heaving.

"Sure."

She came closer and gestured toward the stall. "Can I?"

He nodded. "Of course, take a look."

She peered over the stall and he watched her face light up when she spotted the gangly colt nuzzling his mother's flank. "Oh, he's so adorable. What's his name?"

Mitch half shrugged. "Fluffy."

He saw her smile fractionally and tied the hay net onto the door, and Dolly moved forward eagerly. He was close to Tess. Close enough that he could pick up the faint trace of her perfume above the scent of horse and hay and sweat, and it reached him on a sensory level.

"You're not serious?" she asked, brows raised.

His mouth curled. "Would you like to do the honors?"

She looked intrigued for a moment, but then her expression flattened. "Not my business."

"Is that your way of avoiding the inevitable?" he enquired, and locked the stall door.

"Nothing is inevitable."

"We are," he reminded her, and gestured toward her belly. "One unreliable condom saw to that."

She sucked in a breath. "I'm not going to… I'm not about to…"

"Marry me?" he said when her words trailed off. "Sure you will."

She glared at him. "Sometimes you are an arrogant ass, Mitch. I'm *not* going to marry you. I *don't* love you. You *don't* love me. What we had is over."

"What we *had*," he said harshly, flinching inwardly at the way she could dismiss their past so easily, "doesn't matter one iota. We're having a child together… That's all that matters, Tess. A child who needs both his parents."

"He'll have *both* his parents," she assured him. "Just not living in the same house. And definitely not married."

"Then, as I said earlier, I want shared custody," he shot back.

She made an irritated sound. "Are we back to that again. It's not feasible. I'll be living in town and you can see as much of the baby as you—"

"Half," he said again. "And no compromise."

"That's your problem," she said, clearly annoyed. "You won't compromise on anything. You never would."

"I guess we're both stubborn and uncompromising," he said. He grabbed his shirt from the peg by the stall door and shouldered into it as he took a few steps. "Maybe we should have put *that* on the divorce papers."

He headed for the entrance and heard her pacing after him. "We're not done, Mitch. We need to work this out."

"After lunch," he said, throwing the words over his shoulder. "You're invited, of course."

"I'm not staying for lunch," she huffed, and met him by the door. "Stop being so damned bossy."

He grinned. "Part of my charm," he said, and noticed a car barreling up the driveway. A vehicle he recognized instantly. "Joss is here."

She frowned. "Does he usually—"

"No," he said quickly. "Ellie called him." As his brother's familiar tow truck pulled up outside the house, Mitch spotted another car turning in through the gates. "And Hank."

"What?"

"His patrol car just turned off into the driveway."

She was still frowning. "Two of your brothers? Are we having a family reunion?"

"They're probably just curious and want to see you."

Her mouth curled. "Great. The return of the evil ex."

"My brothers care about you," he reminded her, and began to walk from the stables.

"I know." She sighed. "But I know they blame me for the way things worked out."

"They blame *me*," he assured her. "They think I should have done anything to make you stay."

The truth, he thought. Mitch was always compelled to tell the truth. Maybe it was a throwback to Billie-Jack and his father's inability to be honest about anything except how much he loved liquor. Whatever the reason, Mitch had always wanted to be a better man than Billie-Jack and mostly believed he was. Except for his relationship with Tess. It was his one failure. The one thing he hadn't been able to do successfully.

But fate, it seemed, had given him the opportunity for a do-over.

And he intended to take it.

Tess had always liked Mitch's brothers. Particularly Joss and Hank. They were identical twins, although Hank was taller and broader and had a scar down the left side of his face from a car accident when he was fourteen. Joss, who wore his hair longer and pulled back in a ponytail, was the charmer and an easygoing man who had a likable manner and clearly adored his two young daughters. He was also a widower and owned his own auto repair shop in town. Hank was the chief of police, a role he'd had for a few years. He was rock-solid and the kind of person to go to in a crisis. Mitch had done an amazing job at steering his younger siblings into adulthood.

He would, she realized, make an incredible father.

Of course she'd always known he would be a wonderful parent. It was part of the reason she'd fallen in love with him so many years ago. There was an elemental strength about Mitch. He was a no-nonsense kind of man…honest and driven by a kind of innate integrity she suspected had something to do with his father bailing on the family at a crucial moment in time. But Mitch hadn't failed them. He'd fought to keep the kids together and won the right when he was eighteen.

Loving him had been easy. Until it had all started to go wrong.

And now she was back.

It was like someone had flicked a rewind switch on her life and she was stepping into her old footprints. It was too much to think about, but the memories were acute.

When they were first dating, Mitch had taught her how to ride, and Tess had discovered a love of the land she never knew she possessed. There was something elementally peaceful about being on horseback, with the sun on her arms and the breeze gently touching her face. Often, they would ride around the ranch and find a secluded spot, tether the horses to a tree and then lay down a blanket, for making out or making love. The memory pierced her through to the core. Once, a lifetime ago, loving Mitch had been as essential to her as breathing. Leaving him had been the most difficult thing she had ever done...but necessary. A marriage based on ultimatums wasn't what she wanted—but there was no reasoning with Mitch.

By the time her resolve returned, they were halfway across the yard. Tess did a couple of double steps to match his stride. She grasped his arm and he stopped, looking down.

"What?" he asked.

"Please don't say anything to them about us...you know..."

"Getting married again? Too late," he said quietly. "I think Ellie has already let that cat out of the bag."

She frowned. "We're not getting married, Mitch... and I don't want to have an argument with you about it in front of your family. All I want is for us to be civil and come to an arrangement about the baby."

"We will," he said. Tess suspected she should have felt reassured, but she didn't.

"We'll talk about this later."

"Right," he said, and grabbed her hand. "Later."

Tess was about to snap something out in response, but Joss came toward her, arms outstretched. "Hey, Tess, it's great to see you."

Tess untangled her fingers from Mitch's hand, quickly

hugged his brother and then stepped back. "You, too. How are the girls?" she asked.

"Good, at school and staying at the in-law's tonight," he replied, and grinned, eyes widening as he took in her protruding belly. "I see you've been busy."

She smiled, faintly embarrassed by his teasing. "A little. I guess you...know."

He nodded. "Ellie called," he confirmed, and winked just as Hank moved around the car.

"I suppose there was no point in telling her not to call you," she said and frowned.

"Nope," Joss replied. "You know Brat," he said and grinned again, using the nickname she suspected they still affectionately used for their much-loved little sister.

She nodded and hugged Hank and, once they were done getting reacquainted, Mitch said he needed to get cleaned up, so they all headed for the house. Ellie and Mrs. Bailey were still in the kitchen, busy preparing lunch, and Tess took a seat at the table.

Surreal.

It was the only word that fit. The only thing that made sense.

Tess watched as her former family laughed and chatted and pitched in to prepare the food they were about to eat. They were all clearly curious about her sudden reappearance and pregnancy and asked a few questions, although nothing too probing. She figured Mitch had somehow instructed his brothers to keep their enquiry to a minimum. Even Ellie was a little more subdued than she had been earlier that afternoon, maybe the result of Mitch's directive to quell her enthusiasm for all things that had to do with babies and marriage.

She'd texted her own sister earlier and said she'd be arriving later than expected and would message once she'd left the Triple C. Annie's responding texts had been full of surprise and query, and Tess knew she had a lot of explaining to do once she came face-to-face with her stepsister.

"So, Mitch said you're moving back to town?" Hank enquired quietly.

Tess nodded. "That's the plan. It's a safe town, after all."

"It is on his watch," Joss said, and grinned. "Crime rate has never been lower."

"That's because you've grown up and aren't wreaking havoc," his brother returned. "Joss is very civilized these days…none of that boyhood hell-raising anymore."

Joss laughed. "We all know Lara civilized me." His expression revealed melancholy. They all knew how much he had adored the wife he had lost to a swift and aggressive form of cancer many years earlier. "These days I'm quite the pillar of the community."

"Business owner, member of the local chamber of commerce, former PTA president at the local elementary school. Yep," Hank teased, "you are extraordinary."

Tess smiled at the brothers' banter. They had the strong bond of twins, and were also clearly best friends. It made her happier knowing she'd returned to town and would be able to spend time with her stepsister. She'd missed Annie so much over the past few years, although her sister had visited her in Sioux Falls several times. She was grateful her child would have such a loving aunt and she was grateful for Joss and Hank, too. They would both be wonderful uncles and great role models for her son.

"Yeah, Mr. Chief of Police," Joss teased. "Glad you can recognize greatness in your midst."

"My humble brother has become quite the real estate magnate, too," Hank said with mock disapproval. "How many places do you own now?"

Joss shrugged. "A few. I like to keep busy," he explained, and tugged uncomfortably at his collar.

Everyone laughed, and Tess thought how nice it was to spend time with people whose company she had always enjoyed. The Culhanes were good people, and Mitch had done a wonderful job at raising his siblings.

"So, when's the wedding?"

It was Joss who spoke. Joss, who was watching her over the rim of a beer bottle. Joss, who had clearly decided to disregard the warning she knew Mitch would have dished out.

Tess took a calming breath. "We're not—"

"When we make that decision," she heard her ex-husband respond quietly. "You'll be the first to know."

Tess turned her head and spotted Mitch standing in the doorway, freshly showered, wearing dark jeans and a long-sleeved black T-shirt, and looking effortlessly masculine and so gorgeous she had to catch her breath. His dark hair gleamed. His green eyes glittered. He was everything she remembered—too sexy for words. Strong. Intense. Everything she'd once loved. And now the father of her child. But she wasn't going to get swept up in memories of the life they'd once shared. The past couldn't be changed or erased, and their history was too complicated to simply latch on to the moment and pretend it hadn't happened.

Lunch was soon served and Mitch sat next to Tess, while Ellie took a spot to her left and chatted endlessly about the ranch and her studies and how thrilled she was that the new foal would be staying on the Culhane ranch. Mitch briefly explained about Ramon Alvarez and his investment in the Triple C, to which Ellie responded with a tale about how the man once had mistaken her for a ranch hand.

"I still don't have to like him." Ellie grimaced. "No matter how good his horses are."

"You protest too much," Joss remarked as he helped himself to a hefty serving of lasagna. "And you know what they say about that."

Tess listened as they bantered, with both Joss and Hank taking turns to make fun of their sister and teasing her about crushing on her sworn enemy. Mitch was quiet and concentrated on his food, but she felt him watching her. They had always had a kind of unspoken connection— a way of communicating with very few words. Nothing had changed on that score. Divorce hadn't dissolved their awareness of one another. In fact, Tess suspected the time apart had actually amplified it.

Once lunch was done, they all pitched in to clean up, since Mrs. Bailey had retired to her own cabin before they'd sat down to eat. But not before she'd made Tess promise they would have a real chance to catch up very soon. It wasn't long before Ellie, Joss and Hank headed for the front living room and Tess was left drying the last of the dishes while Mitch put the plates and cutlery away.

"This is cozy."

She looked sideways, saw he was watching her and felt her spine straighten automatically. "No, it's ridiculous. I really should go home."

"Home?"

"Well, to Annie's."

One brow cocked up. "That's not your home."

"It will be for the moment," she replied, folding the tea towel, startled by how familiar the chore of standing in Mitch's kitchen, doing dishes, actually felt. "Until I find my own place. And stop being such a control freak."

"Habit," he quipped. "I don't want you living at my cousins'."

"Not your business."

His gaze shifted to her middle. "You think?"

"This is a baby, Mitch, not property or a head of cattle or a new colt. You are this baby's father, but you don't own this child. Or me. You don't make my decisions for me."

He didn't react to her veiled insult. Instead, he closed the pantry door and sighed impatiently "Can I at least help you find somewhere to live?"

"Which means, can you pay for it, right? Then, no... you can't. I have enough money saved to support myself until the baby comes, and then I intend going back to work part-time. I've already enquired at a couple of the local schools." She saw his expression darken, clearly frustrated, and she sighed. "Look, I'm not deliberately trying to be difficult, but I didn't come here to step back into my old life. I returned to Cedar River to have the baby, to offer you involvement with our child. And I genuinely want that, Mitch."

"But on your terms," he said, his gaze narrowing. "Right?"

Tess shrugged slightly. "I'm happy to meet you halfway."

"If that were true," he shot back, "you'd be upstairs in our old room, unpacking your bags."

"And slipping right back into our old life, correct?"

"Would that be so bad?"

"We're divorced," she reminded him. "Remember? And the reason we got divorced still exists."

"The reason we got divorced doesn't matter now," he said. "Because we have a baby coming and our child deserves to be raised by us both, *equally, in this house*."

"That's impossible."

"Then why did you come back, Tess?" he asked impatiently. "Why involve me at all if you're so set on doing everything on your own terms?"

Tess swallowed hard. She knew he had a point and a real argument regarding her motives, but she wasn't about to cave. She had to maintain her resolve. She was back in Cedar River, but not back in Mitch's life.

"I want my child to have his father in his life. But that's it, Mitch. *His* life, not mine. I have to concentrate on the baby," she replied. "After everything that happened, I need to make sure I carry him to full term… It's all I have time for, Mitch," she said, her voice betraying her emotion, her finger touching her temple. "In here."

He reached out, tracing a finger along her jaw and settling at her chin. His touch was familiar, but she still flinched. His gaze darkened instantly, and Tess swallowed hard. She didn't want to feel so aware of him, so easily mesmerized by his touch. But memory took her hostage and she stood in silence, watching him, feeling the heat emanate from his strong frame.

"I know that," he said. "I understand, Tess. I know how much you want this baby and I don't want to upset you or make things difficult. I just want—"

"I know what you want." She pulled away and stepped back. "You want me to agree with everything you say and move back in and pretend that all the hurt and pain we caused one another four years ago didn't happen. But I can't do that, Mitch. It did happen. *We were broken.* We're still broken. What happened between us in that hotel room six months ago hasn't changed our past… It only changed our future."

He looked at her—deep into that place only he could reach. And for a crazy moment Tess longed for things to be different, for the past to be erased and for their present to be filled with everything they had lost. But wishes were for fools. She had to maintain her position for the sake of her baby.

"I have to go," she said, and pushed back her shoulders.

"We haven't finished this—"

"I'll let you know when I find my own place," she said, cutting him off. "I'll be staying with Annie until then."

She grabbed her bag and marched out of the room, feeling the intensity of his gaze burning through her as she walked. She ducked into the living room on her way out and said a brief farewell to his brothers and Ellie, and a few minutes later she was in her car and heading down the driveway.

And away from Mitch.

But they weren't done...not by a long shot.

"You look like you need to talk."

Mitch was in the living room with Hank and Joss, as Ellie had bailed and headed back to her cottage once Tess had left. He sat in the chaise by the window, staring at the untouched beer in his hand, legs stretched out and feet crossed at the ankles. He glanced toward Hank, who made the observation, and shrugged.

"Are you sure the baby is yours?" Joss asked bluntly.

Mitch's gaze sharpened. "Tess doesn't lie."

"I wasn't suggesting she—"

"It's mine. I can..." His words trailed off and he tapped his knuckles to his chest briefly. "I can feel it. Don't ask me how... I just know. And Tess has no reason to falsely claim the baby is mine. Frankly, I'm sure she'd prefer he was someone else's, considering our history."

"He?" Joss's brows shot up.

Mitch shrugged. "We're not sure, but Tess seems to think it's a boy. But I'd be equally happy if it's a girl. The baby will be here in a few months, and even though

I've barely had a few hours to get my head around the idea, I can't wait."

Joss smiled and for a moment his brother looked lost in his thoughts. "I understand what you mean. I love being a dad," he admitted. "It's the best thing I've ever done. And you've had a lot of practice raising us hellions, so I know you're gonna be great at it."

Mitch's chest tightened. "Thanks."

"What about Tess?" Hank asked. "Ellie said you guys were getting married again?"

He shrugged. "It's the obvious thing to do."

"But?"

"She's intent on raising the baby alone—with me *involved*..." Mitch made exasperated air quotes around the word. "And she won't listen to reason."

"Reason meaning," Hank suggested, "you want to get married again, and she doesn't think it's a good idea?"

Mitch nodded and expelled a heavy breath. "I want to raise my child where he or she deserves to be raised... here, on this ranch. I want my son or daughter to grow up as a Culhane, and marrying Tess will make that happen."

"But she hates you, right?" Joss remarked, one brow cocked.

Mitch shrugged again. "Hate? I don't know. We have a lot of water under the bridge. A lot of blame and recrimination. We parted badly. And the thing in Sioux Falls—I don't know... It was almost like we were finally saying goodbye to one another. Only..."

"You knocked her up?" Joss remarked, still grinning.

He glared at his brother. "Don't talk about Tess like that."

"I'm kidding," Joss said, and waved a hand. "And just checking for your reaction. Are you still in love with her?"

"No," Mitch replied quickly, hating the way his chest tightened. Because he wasn't sure what he felt for Tess. He'd had years of built-up resentment to crush any feelings of love he'd once had. When she had walked out he'd forced himself to stop loving her. The physical thing had been harder to let go—it was just chemistry—a straight-up sexual attraction that was about pheromones and desire and had little to do with actual feelings. That's why they'd hooked up in Sioux Falls. Plain and simple sex, which had turned into a complication neither of them had expected. "It's not about that. It's about what's best."

"You can't force her to get married, though," Hank said. "Or move back in. So, what are you going to do?"

"Use good old logic to convince her that getting married again is the best possible solution."

Joss laughed. "No offense, big brother, but that's a lose-lose plan."

Mitch scowled. "What?"

"She isn't gonna be thinking about anything other than her baby," Joss replied, still laughing, but softer this time, as though he was lost in a memory. "I remember when Lara was pregnant, she went all lioness. Nothing else mattered but the baby she carried—and rightly so. It's like their protective instincts go into overdrive. You start talking about logic and legacy and doing *what's right*, and Tess will be all over that logic and have it for an afternoon snack. You've been through this before," his brother reminded him. "Don't you remember?"

That was true. But this was the first time Tess had carried a child past sixteen weeks. During their first pregnancy, they'd shared the excitement, planning their life with their baby. The second time was harder—they were both on edge, waiting and wondering and hoping she wouldn't miscarry. When they lost their second child,

Mitch tried to help Tess grieve but always seemed to come up short. After that, he shut down, felt like a robot, almost feeling nothing because the reality of what they endured was too awful to bear.

"The truth is," he admitted wearily. "I'm scared to death."

"Understandable," Joss replied and nodded. "You guys went through a lot back then and now Tess is pregnant again, you're bound to have some fear and anxiety. Just don't let that turn you into a self-righteous horse's ass about the whole thing."

Mitch scowled. "Really?"

Joss nodded and grinned. "You have been known to think you have all the answers." He paused and waved a hand. "I don't know… Get back to basics."

"Basics?" Mitch echoed.

"Yeah," the other man replied. "Take off your I'm-in-charge-of-everything-and-everyone hat and work the angle you do have."

"Which is?"

"She was in love with you once," Joss said. "Get her to fall in love with you again."

Mitch winced. That was impossible. On her last day at the ranch, Tess had made her feelings toward him abundantly clear. She didn't love him anymore. She never wanted to see him again. He was the last man in the world she wanted to be married to. Or have a child with.

We were broken.

Her words came back with painful clarity. Because she was right. They had become as distant as two people could be. The love they had once shared, the love that he'd believed would bind them together forever, had disappeared almost as though it had never existed.

"We lost what we had," he said flatly, tired of the conversation. What did his brothers really know? As far as he knew, Hank had never had a serious relationship and Joss bounced from one meaningless one-night stand to the next trying the erase the pain of losing his wife. He got to his feet and stared at his brothers. "I have work to do."

"Don't get worked up just because you know I'm right," Jose said. "What have you got to lose?"

Pride...

"I can't," he said, and shrugged.

"A hundred bucks says you can," Joss shot back, and laughed.

Mitch left the room and headed outside, grateful for the rush of fresh air into his lungs as he strode across the yard. The clear sky, the scent of animals and earth, fueled him like nothing else could, and he relaxed a little with each step.

Tess.

Their baby.

It had been a long morning and Mitch thought his head might explode.

But the more he walked, the more he thought Joss might be right. Handing out ultimatums to Tess wouldn't work. He needed to change tactics. He needed a plan.

She'd loved him once.

Maybe she could again.

A date. First one, and then another. Just spending time together. Until he could remind her of all the reasons they'd been happy together once—and could be again, this time as the family they'd always wanted.

Easy. Foolproof.

Mitch stared up at the sky and laughed ruefully.

I am officially screwed.

Chapter Four

Despite the turmoil churning through her blood, Tess was glad to be back in Cedar River. The McCall ranch was much smaller than the Triple C and was more like a hobby farm than a ranch, but the place felt like a real home. The best part was hanging out with her stepsister, Annie.

Years ago, when Tess was nine and Annie was eight, her mother had married Annie's father and they had quickly formed a bond, as close as sisters could be. Their parents had moved to Wyoming over a decade ago to be close to her stepfather's elderly parents, and she still kept in regular contact with them, although she hadn't told them about the baby just yet. But she knew they would be delighted they were about to become grandparents. When Annie began working for David, Tess had voiced her concerns—David might have the McCall surname, but he was *still* a Culhane. David's mother was Mitch's aunt. Although Sandra had died in a plane crash several years ago, alongside David's wife, she was certain Sandra McCall had lost contact with her younger brother the moment he'd bailed on his family. Sandra's husband, Ivan, never discussed Billie-Jack or his deceased wife's relationship with her brother.

"So," her sister queried as they sat in the living room and sipped tea. "Do you want to talk about it?"

Tess looked at her sister and shrugged. "Not really."

She'd given Annie a brief rundown of Mitch's reaction to the baby the day before, excluding the part about Mitch insisting they get remarried, because she knew Annie was a romantic at heart and would want to know *everything*, including Tess's reasons for not agreeing to move back to the ranch. That aside, she was grateful that her sister wasn't quick to hand out judgment about her decision. And, as expected, her sister was very happy for her. She was the only person beside Mitch who knew how much she had grieved the loss of her babies.

"What are you going to do?" Annie asked gently.

Tess shrugged lightly. "Find my own place. Have the baby. Get a job. Live my life. You know, the usual stuff."

"And Mitch?"

"He can be as involved as he wants."

Now Annie looked a little skeptical. "Are you sure? I mean, I know how angry you still are at Mitch and—"

"I'm not angry at him," she cut in quickly. "I want my child to have his father in his life and I know Mitch will be an excellent dad. But anything else is out of the question."

"Anything else?" her sister quizzed. "So…" Annie's voice trailed off for a second. "When you hooked up in Sioux Falls… What was that?"

Heat crawled up her neck and she shrugged a fraction. "Just…chemistry."

"And it didn't mean anything?"

She swallowed hard. "Well, of course it meant *something*... I mean, Mitch and I have a lot of history. But not all of it is good. We've always had a strong physical connection... I guess what happened when we met again was inevitable because of that. But," she added firmly, "that's over now. I am not going to spend any time pining over my attraction to him. I'm only thinking about the future, and my baby's future."

Annie looked at her and sighed heavily. "Well, you can stay here as long as you like. There's plenty of room and I love having you here."

Tess glanced around. Her sister had occupied the guest house on the McCall ranch since she'd taken the position as nanny to David McCall's children, who were now four and eight. David's wife had died when their youngest child was only six months old and, after a series of unsuitable nannies, Annie had started working at the ranch. Tess knew the kids adored her. David owned an accountancy practice in town and worked long hours, so Annie was with the kids weekdays, and she had most weekends to herself unless her boss had other arrangements. Tess also knew her sister wasn't happy and wanted to leave her job, but the affection she had for David's kids kept her from quitting. As, Tess suspected, did the feelings she also had for David.

"I know," Tess said warmly as she sipped the tea her sister had made. "But the sooner I find a place of my own, the better. I only want something small. And hopefully close to town."

Annie nodded and checked her watch. "David's working at the office for a few hours this morning so I'm going to watch the kids, but we can talk again a little later, okay?"

"Sure. I think I'll check out the local real estate listings and afterwards read a book for a while."

"Good idea. No overdoing things," Annie chastised gently. "And I love having you here, by the way."

Once Annie left for the main house, Tess ate some cereal, managing to keep down more than usual, and then took a shower and got dressed. Afterward, she grabbed her electronic tablet, and found a comfortable spot in the small living room. She sat lotus style on the couch and started checking out the local real estate listings, while she sipped on more tea and avoided thinking about her ex-husband.

Which was impossible, since he turned up on the doorstep at around nine o'clock.

He was dressed in his regulation jeans, chambray shirt, sheepskin-lined jacket and cowboy boots. His hair was tousled, like he'd been running his hand through it as he waited for her to answer the door.

"I went to the main house," he said as she cranked open the door. "Your sister said you were here. Can we talk?"

For a moment she considered telling him to come back later, then realized she had no real reason to send him away.

"Okay, come in." She stepped back to allow him across the threshold.

He followed her down the short hallway and she pointed to the living room.

Once they were seated, he spoke. "How are you feeling this morning?"

"I'm fine," she replied. "I slept well."

He linked his hands together. "Do you need to see a doctor regularly?" he asked quietly. "In light of your history."

Tess nodded. "I will. In fact, I have an appointment with a new obstetrician in Rapid City next week."

"I'd like to come with you."

Tess wasn't surprised by his request and could think of no valid reason to refuse. "Sure," she said casually. "We can find out the sex of the baby if you like."

"If that's what you want. I'm happy either way."

She nodded. "I think I'd like to know. I'll let you know the day and time."

He let out a heavy breath and she noticed he looked tired, as though he hadn't slept much. Not surprising, she supposed, after what had transpired between them the day before. It was a lot to digest. All things he couldn't control. Which she knew would drive him out of his mind.

"I want to apologize for the way I acted yesterday," he said. "I was in shock, I guess. And with the family there, I may have said a few things that—"

"You were a total jerk," she remarked, and crossed her arms. "But since I *did* arrive unexpectedly and told you about the baby…you're off the hook for being an idiot."

His mouth twitched. "Thanks."

"So…anything else?"

"I wanted to see you." He shrugged. "Just to make sure you were okay."

"I'm fine," she replied, trying not to care that he was worried about her. "In fact, I was planning on heading into town to check out some real estate listings, so I should probably—"

"I'll go with you," he said, jumping to his feet.

Tess shook her head instantly. "That's not a good—"

"I want to help, Tess. It's the least you can let me do."

Of course he did. Typical Mitch. "I don't suppose there's any point in me refusing?"

"Nope."

Tess stood and took a long breath. "I'll just get my coat and bag."

She was walking toward his truck a few minutes later, after sending Annie a brief text message saying she was heading out with Mitch for a while. Her sister responded with a surprised emoji, and while Tess wanted to send a snippy reply about Annie's crush on her employer, she had enough troubles without involving herself in her sister's drama.

"Are you warm enough?" Mitch asked once they were settled inside his Ranger.

She nodded. "Like toast."

He started the ignition. "That's a good idea."

She looked sideways. "What is?"

"Breakfast."

"I've already had breakfast."

"I haven't," he said.

"Surely Mrs. B wouldn't let you out of the house without feeding you first."

She saw his grin. "I had an early meeting with Grady Parker. We're both brand inspectors for the county."

Tess knew Grady. He was a local rancher and probably Mitch's number-one competitor when it came to horse breeding and training. Still, she knew the men were more allies than rivals.

"I don't think breakfast is a good idea," she said. "And I don't think—"

"We need to talk," he said. "We can either do it here, at the ranch or over a meal. I'd prefer to be civil about this, Tess."

Civil? Right.

"Fine," she said, looking straight ahead. "Whatever."

The drive into town was tense, mostly because Tess was silently cursing him for being an arrogant know-it-all who believed he was entitled to get whatever he wanted simply because he had an insatiable need to be in command of everything and everyone around him. Even though she, perhaps more than anyone else, understood why he was who he was, it still made her crazy.

Once they reached Main Street, he spoke. "Where would you like to go? O'Sullivan's?"

She nodded, and within minutes they were pulling into the parking area outside the hotel.

The restaurant was as busy as expected for a Saturday morning, but they got a table, and within minutes a waitress approached and took their order. Tess settled on tea and then decided she was hungry, so she ordered a short pancake stack, while Mitch ordered eggs and coffee.

"So, what do you want to talk about?" she asked calmly.

He eased back in the chair. "You're not serious?"

"Perfectly."

He was quiet for a moment, then spoke. "You look nice today. That color suits you."

Tess glanced down at her blue woolen dress. Their drinks arrived and she spooned a little sugar into her tea. She looked at him, noticing how the tiny pulse in his cheek throbbed, and knew he was trying very hard to appear as though they were simply having a casual and no-pressure interaction. She wasn't fooled. Mitch was smart and would have spent the last twenty-four hours trying to figure out a way to get her to do what he wanted.

Like get married again.

Which was never going to happen.

"What?" He frowned, as though he knew what she was thinking.

"Stop looking so innocent," she replied. "I'm onto you, Culhane. You're acting all civilized and charming...but I know you're trying to figure a way to get what you want."

His mouth twitched. "And what is it you think I want?"

"Your own way," she replied, her expression humorless.

"I know you, Mitch. You can take me to breakfast, tell me I look nice, ask me how I'm feeling...but I know you have an agenda. You think we should get married again."

"Of course I do."

"And I don't," she said, and sipped her tea. "We're divorced. And the reasons we got divorced are still there."

"And the baby?" he asked.

"We talked about this yesterday, Mitch," she replied, feeling the tension rise in her belly. The last thing she wanted was a rehash of the previous day's conversation. But they needed to clear the air. "I've never planned on denying you the chance to be a father to our child and you can see as much of the baby as you want. But that's it. You and I are over...for good."

Mitch watched his ex-wife as she spoke, his gaze focused on her mouth and the tightness in her jaw. Resentment and irritation churned in his gut. And something else. An awareness fueled by memory...by all they had once been to one another...and then all they had lost.

He eased back in his seat. "You know that a good lawyer would get me fifty-fifty custody, right?"

Her shoulders tensed. "Is that your plan? To get a lawyer."

"No," he replied stiffly, thinking that perhaps he should have a discreet conversation with his neighbor, Tyler Madden, who was a lawyer and had a practice in town. "But I have as much invested here as you do, Tess. The child inside you *is* as much mine as yours. And has a right to my name and the legacy that is his or hers by birthright."

"Our child will have it, I promise," she said quietly. "We don't have to live together or be married to successfully co-parent, Mitch."

"You know a lot about parenting then?"

It was a sharp-edged dig, but he was annoyed and couldn't help it. He saw her expression turn into a scowl. But she had no real idea what she was asking of him— to simply sit on the sidelines and take whatever crumbs she allowed.

"I'll learn," she replied stiffly. "Like you had to when you gained custody of your siblings."

It was a fair call. And a good comeback. She certainly had added gumption to her game since they'd broken up. The Tess he once knew—the Tess he'd once loved—she was a lot more easygoing and they never fought or spoke to one another in anger—until the end of their marriage. He didn't like how arrogant and entitled that made him feel. But the truth was that over the years Mitch had gotten used to things going his own way. And until Tess had moved out and divorced him, he'd managed to steer his own ship with little resistance from his brothers and sister, or anyone else. The way Billie-Jack had bailed on them and then signed over custody had taught Mitch that he needed to stand firm in what he wanted, even if he acted like some kind of self-important ass in the process. Family came first. And his child—the one growing in Tess's belly—had the right to everything he could give him or her.

"What did you think I would do, Tess?" he asked. "Sit back and let you make all the rules?"

"I had hoped you'd be reasonable and fair."

"Do you think it's unreasonable that I want to raise my child on the ranch that is his or her legacy?"

"*Our* child," she said pointedly. "And no, of course not. But we have to share the parenting, Mitch. On equal terms. Not *your* way. Not *my* way. But *our* way."

"That might be difficult since you're the one with all the rules."

She sat back abruptly in her seat and stared at him for a moment before her expression softened. "I suppose it seems that way."

"Seems?" he queried.

She expelled a heavy breath. "Okay, so perhaps you're not the only one with control issues. I'll stop being so bossy, but I need you to stop doing something, too."

"And what's that?"

She looked directly at him. "You have to stop insisting we can have some kind of happily-ever-after. Because frankly, neither of us want that, right?"

"We loved each other once," he reminded her, looking for some indication that she remembered all they had been to each other. Talking about old feelings stirred up something he'd tried valiantly to put out of his thoughts years ago. "I thought that might have been enough for you to give us another chance."

She stared at him. "It's not."

He winced inwardly. "Do you hate me that much?"

She took a breath. "I don't hate you. I hated what we became."

He understood. They'd said a lot of harsh things to one another. Things they couldn't take back. Still, Mitch wasn't going to be swayed. Their child deserved better.

"We can't raise our child apart, Tess," he said. "He needs us both...full-time."

She shook her head. "There's no other way."

"There is," he said, and sighed impatiently, thinking he needed to try another angle. "If you don't want to get married again, fair enough. But at least move back to the ranch so we can both be there for our child."

"You're not listening," she said, her voice a whisper. "I'm not interested in a reconciliation, Mitch."

"I'm not talking about *us*," he said, and then waited a moment once their food was served and the waitress disappeared. "I'm talking about our baby. He or she needs two parents...living together, as a family."

She inhaled, her nostrils flaring. "Say I do move back to the ranch. What then?" she asked. "What do you imagine that looks like? Separate rooms? Separate lives? How does that make our child feel safe and secure? Kids need stability and security and the knowledge that their parents will always be there for them. That doesn't include witnessing a loveless relationship year in and year out. And what happens if one or both of us fall in love with other people? How confusing will that be? I'm not going to do that to my child. Apart is best...it's the only way."

Separate lives? Other people? Loveless relationship? The resolution in her voice twisted behind his ribs like a hot knife. Mitch stared at her, looking for the woman he had once loved and who had once loved him. All he saw was cool determination and an unwillingness to meet him even an inch of the way. She was stubborn and completely unreasonable. She had him exactly where she wanted him...and they both knew it.

"Okay," Mitch said easily, outwardly conceding defeat because he knew from the way she was chewing on her lower lip that there was no point in trying to cajole her or insist she change her mind over breakfast. It would take time. The baby was still months away. He had that advantage, at least, he thought as he pushed his food around on the plate. "Eat up, and we'll go and check out the real estate listings."

Her suspicious look increased tenfold and he watched

as she stabbed at her pancakes and muttered something under her breath.

"What was that?" he asked, smiling to himself.

She glared at him. "You're such a jerk."

Mitch grinned. "Because I want to spend time with you?"

"That's not what you want."

"Sure it is," he said. "Despite how complicated things seem, Tess, the reality is quite simple…we're having a baby. And I'm really happy for us both."

Her eyes glistened and he knew she fought an internal battle with feelings just as he did.

"I'm glad you're happy about the baby, Mitch," she said. "I'm happy, too. All you need to do now is learn to stop telling me what to do."

He chuckled. "I'll do my best. Although, you're a little headstrong yourself, so it goes both ways."

"I'll try," she said and pushed her plate away. "I'm finished. Can we go?"

"Sure," he replied, and got to his feet. He moved around the table and took her hand to help her out of the booth. A familiar and crazy electric current shot up his arm like wildfire. She felt it, too, he was sure, because her head jerked up and she immediately met his gaze. It was still there, still between them. Alchemy. Chemistry. Attraction. The very thing that had brought them together in the first place was as real and as intense as it had ever been. It was what had driven them into each other's arms that afternoon in Sioux Falls…and what had led to them falling in love so many years ago.

She pulled away and grabbed her bag, wasting no time as she walked from the table. Mitch paid the check and met her at the door. The hotel was busy and the foyer bustling with guests and staff. Mitch spotted the owner, Liam

O'Sullivan, by the concierge desk and offered a mild acknowledgment. He'd never liked the O'Sullivans much. They were the wealthiest family in town and owned most of the commercial real estate. But he had to admit that Liam had turned the hotel into one of the best around, and it was certainly good for the local economy.

Mitch caught up with Tess by the door. "Shall we walk to the Realtor's office?" he asked, and then glanced down at her belly. She looked tired, he thought, and suspected she hadn't slept much the night before. Like he hadn't. "It's only one block, but we can drive if walking is too much for you."

"I'm not an invalid," she said tightly. "And stop making the rules. You promised, remember?"

Mitch exhaled. "Don't confuse concern with control, Tess."

"Sometimes with you it's hard to know the difference."

It was another direct dig—another go at how little she thought of him. But he ignored it, because getting worked up about Tess's lack of faith in him or them made him hurt all over.

"Walk or drive?" he asked casually.

"Drive," she replied, and headed for his truck.

Exasperated, Mitch followed and opened the door once he reached the vehicle. "Not everything has to be an argument, Tess."

She met his gaze. "I know. And I don't want to go around and around the same old discussion."

"Okay," he said, way more agreeably than he felt. "How about we park the idea about you moving back to the ranch for the moment?"

"Good plan."

His mouth twitched. "You said you wanted to check out real estate listings."

They got into the truck without another word, and she didn't speak until he'd pulled up outside the real estate office. He scored a parking space and turned off the ignition.

"You don't need to come inside," she said as she unclipped her seat belt.

Mitch was out the door before she could make another protest. He moved around the truck and opened the passenger side.

"Let's go," he said, and ushered her forward.

"I guess there's no point in insisting you stay here, right?"

He shrugged. "Not really."

She shook her head and walked toward the office. The bell above the door dinged as they crossed the threshold, and a woman moved around the counter. A woman they both knew. Leola Jurgens. Real estate agent. And gossip connoisseur. Mitch was well acquainted with the forty-something woman, as he'd schooled two of her daughter's horses, and he knew she would recognize Tess immediately, since his ex-wife had had taught both girls at the local school.

"Well, this certainly is a morning for surprises," Leola said with a grin, and Mitch saw Tess wince. "I never thought I'd see you two back together. And a baby on the way, too," she added dramatically. She grasped Tess's hand, clearly putting the obvious together and making her own assumptions. "Such lovely news."

"Hello, Mrs. Jurgens," Tess said politely, and removed her hand. "I was wondering if I could—"

"Oh, call me Leola," she insisted. "Now, what can I do for you?"

Mitch listened as Tess explained about needing a house to lease, and he felt a swift unease creep up his neck.

He knew Leola Jurgens would be curious, like anyone in town who knew them. People would talk, it was inevitable. Tess was back and she was having his baby, but they wouldn't be living together...at least that's what his ex-wife wanted. It would be enough to get the rumor mills churning. Mitch hated gossip. When Billie-Jack had bailed, Mitch had endured endless comments from acquaintances *and* friends...all telling him that he was crazy to want custody of his younger siblings. Most people thought he should look after himself and allow the youngest kids to go and live with his aunt, Sandra, and farm the older ones out to social services. So he could have his own life, they'd said. So he wouldn't have the worry or the responsibility, they'd said. The talk and unwanted advice had fueled his decision to keep his family together. It had been so hard at first. The younger ones didn't understand what had happened. Jake had internalized his rage toward Billie-Jack. Hank was fighting for his life in the hospital after the car accident that had been their father's catalyst for leaving, while Mitch was commuting back and forth to Rapid City to maintain a vigil beside his brother's hospital bed.

Sometimes he wondered how they all pulled through those first six months. But Mrs. Bailey had helped, and his aunt Sandra and her husband, Ivan. What was left of the Culhanes had closed ranks and they became a strong and united front, and stronger for all the grief and betrayal they had endured. He missed Sandra and the tragedy of losing both her and David's wife, Jayne, was still a raw wound for the whole family.

Lost in memories for a moment, Mitch listened vaguely as Leola prattled on about a few homes she had for rent and offered to show them a couple of places.

"You can come in my car," Leola offered, "or follow in your own."

"Are you okay?" she asked and touched his arm.

Mitch glanced to where her hand lay against his jacket and swallowed hard. "We'll follow," he said.

Leola nodded and minutes later she locked up the office and they walked outside. Once he was back in the truck with Tess, he buckled up and waited while she fiddled with the seat beat. The belt flipped out of her hand and she cursed softly, which made him chuckle. Tess was never one for profanity. Mitch reached across and grabbed the seat belt, drawing it gently across her abdomen, and his palm grazed her belly. She winced and he went to snatch his hand away, but suddenly she rested her own hand over his, holding him steady against her stomach.

"The baby's moving," she said quietly.

Mitch's chest tightened. "For real?"

She nodded and pressed his hand firmer. "Well, it is probably more like fluttering, but it feels…it feels… I guess it feels exactly liked I'd hoped it would."

Mitch stilled, his palm burning where it lay against her rounded belly, and experienced an acute and riveting connection to the woman he'd loved and lost.

"I can feel it," he said softly, looking into her face and regsitering how her eyes glistened.

"We've never had this moment before."

"I know," he whispered and smoothed his palm over her stomach. "It's amazing."

"I want this baby so much, Mitch. I've tried not to worry…not to think about the babies we've lost…but sometimes I can't help it. If anything were to happen…"

"It won't," he assured her when her words trailed off. "You said yourself that this time *feels* different."

"It does," she said and sighed. "But I still—"

"Stop worrying," he said gently, cutting her off. "Let me worry instead. Let me do that for you, at least."

She nodded. "Okay."

"Everything will work out, Tess, I promise," he assured her, feeling the need to offer her whatever comfort he could. So much had transpired between them, so much loss and anguish and despair. But in that moment, as her hand pressed firmly over his, all he felt was a surge of something so intense, so real, he could barely draw a breath.

Hope.

And he knew he'd never really gotten over her.

Then he wondered what the hell he could do about it.

Chapter Five

Tess removed her hand and stared directly ahead. The last thing she wanted was to get caught up in a tender moment with her ex-husband. She had to keep her head. To remember that he had an agenda and would do whatever he had to in order to get what he wanted. And Tess wasn't about to be manipulated into marriage or cohabiting with him...not under any circumstances.

He must have sensed the shift in her mood because he removed his hand and turned in his seat, sighing heavily as he started the vehicle. Tess glanced at him, noticing his hands were tight on the steering wheel, loathing the feelings that were churning inside her. During their years apart, she'd tucked away the memories of how strong and comforting his hands were, how easily her head had fit into the crook of his shoulder, how safe she had felt in his arms. In the small confines of the truck cab, her skin still tingling where his hand had laid against her belly, the intimacy between them had never seemed more real or raw.

She knew she had to stop remembering, stop thinking…stop *overthinking*.

"How long do you think it will be before Leola lets the whole town know I'm back?" she asked, trying to sound casual as they followed the other woman's vehicle as it pulled away from the sidewalk.

"Hours," he replied. "She'll tell Alice from the bakery, Alice will tell old man Radici from the pizza parlor, he'll tell Shirley from the museum and soon it will be old news. So, relax."

"I don't care about a little gossip. People are naturally curious and you're one of the most popular guys around this town," she said, not liking the way that made her feel. Mitch was well-known…and well respected. No doubt she'd become the villain when she divorced him. In fact, she was surprised that the single women in town hadn't started circling the moment she left.

"What?" he asked.

"Huh?" she responded, and glanced at him.

"You huffed."

Tess's skin prickled. "I did not."

"You did. Something on your mind?"

Tess remained silent for about ten seconds. "Why don't you have a girlfriend?"

He eased the truck into the midmorning traffic. "A girlfriend?"

"Partner, lover, significant other," she said with emphasis and turning hot all over. "You know, a woman in your life."

He glanced sideways for a moment, checking out her belly, his mouth tightening. "It would be a little crowded at the moment, don't you think?"

Tess tensed as unwanted emotions flared through her blood. Guilt. Regret. And more feeling than she wanted to acknowledge. "I don't want to be the reason that you don't share your life with someone."

"That's not your call, is it?" he shot back, and took a left turn off Main Street.

"What does that mean?"

"It means that relationships are messy and can't be made to order. It means that I wasn't in any fit state to be with anyone else after you left, and now it's all moot because you're here and you're having my baby, and we have to work out a way to try and *not* screw this up for our child's sake." He turned into Reed Street and pulled up behind Leola's Subaru. "We're here."

He was out of the truck in seconds and came around to her side. Tess got out and met Leola by the gate.

"Since you're looking for a a rental, I suppose you're not moving into the Culhane ranch?" Leola asked, brows raised inquisitively.

"That's correct. But I'm happy to take a short-term lease," she added, trying to avoid giving the other woman too much information. "Who knows what the future will hold."

Leola offered a nervy kind of laugh and nodded, standing back to let them pass through the gate as Mitch came up behind her and gently guided her by the elbow. Tess relaxed a little, finding a familiar comfort in his closeness.

The house was old and small, but the yard was neat and fully fenced. Leola opened the front door and invited them inside.

"This is a dump," he said bluntly, once they were inside and walking down the narrow hallway.

"Mitch," she chastised, keeping her voice low. "Be nice."

True, it wasn't a palace, but if she ignored the peeling wallpaper, shabby decor and musty smell, it had good bones and would look much better with some fresh paint. "It's not that bad."

"Ah… I'll just leave you alone while you look around," Leola said and walked toward the front door.

Once the other woman was out of range, he flicked a little peeling paint off the wall. "I won't allow—"

"Allow?" Tess jerked her hands to her hip. "Can you actually hear yourself when you speak?"

He managed to look apologetic. "I'd *prefer* our child didn't live in a place like this. I don't mean to be—"

"Sure you do," she said, cutting him off again. "I'll give you some latitude, Mitch, but I won't be told what I can do, or where I can do it."

He nodded agreeably. "Okay. But there are mold spores in the ceiling. It's not safe."

She glanced up, squinting to see if she could spot the spores, and couldn't. Still, the more she looked around, the less the shabby house appealed to her. "Okay, we'll go to the next place."

The next home, one about five streets away, was larger and two stories. Too dangerous, Mitch said, for her to try to maneuver a stroller up and down a flight of stairs. The third house was no better, in his exalted opinion. There were bars on the windows, which he informed her made the place a firetrap. And was totally unsuitable for their child.

"The previous owners were a little paranoid about security," Leola explained when Tess asked about the bars. "I have suggested to the current owner that they be removed to make the place more appealing. I can find out for you if you like?"

Tess nodded. "Sure, thank you."

"Is there anything else?" Mitch asked as they walked back to their vehicles.

"Not today," Leola replied, her lips pressed together. "I'll be in touch. Where can I contact you?"

Tess gave Leola her cell number and they remained by the truck as the Realtor got into her car and drove off. Once the vehicle was out of sight, Tess turned her attention to her ex-husband.

"Could you have been any more painful?"

"What did I say?" he asked, looking innocent.

Tess huffed. "Seriously? Mold spores? Firetrap? You weren't exactly looking to like."

"I only want you and the baby to be safe."

It was a nice story, but she didn't completely believe it. "Maybe that's a part of it, but the other part is you trying to control things, and we both know it."

"Okay," he said, suddenly infuriatingly agreeable. "How about we go back to the ranch and you can check out which room you'd like me to set up as a nursery?" He paused for a moment, clearly waiting on her reaction. "For when the baby stays with me, of course."

Oh, he was clever. "Of course," she said stiffly.

"Is that a yes?"

She shrugged, thinking she should probably go directly back to her sister's place, but knew that Mitch would be relentless. And it would give her another chance, if need be, to make her plans abundantly clear. Not that she wanted to rehash the same old argument, but Mitch wasn't a man to be easily swayed by her refusals. She knew that from experience. "Sure, let's go. I'd like to see Dolly's foal again."

They were back on the road a few moments later. The weather was overcast, and Mitch commented that they were predicting an early snowfall for the coming season.

"Annie was saying they'd opened up the recreational park below Kegg's Mountain again for the tourists," she said casually, keen to steer the conversation away from anything to do with her finding somewhere to live, even though she knew Mitch wouldn't let up on the idea of her moving back to the ranch.

He nodded. "Yeah, it's been a few months since they've allowed tourists and campers into the park. Too many landslides," he added. "The mountain keeps rumbling and several of the old copper mines have become unstable. Seems okay now, though."

"Do you still volunteer for the emergency services?"

Mitch was renowned for being one of the best trackers in the district and was often called out to help search for lost tourists in the busy holiday season.

"When they need me. I haven't had to go out for a while, which is good. And Shanook is getting a little old for it now. I might have to train a new dog if I keep at it."

She knew he and the old wolfhound were an amazing search-and-rescue team. "Do you hear much from Jake?" she asked.

He shrugged. "He calls every couple of months. You know Jake… He's never been one for keeping in touch."

She did know it. She also knew Mitch missed his brother. "He's out of the military now?"

"Yes. He's working in security with a buddy of his from the army…high-end computer stuff. It all goes over my head," he said, and grinned. "I can barely use a smart phone."

Tess chuckled, recalling that Mitch wasn't one for technology. Oh, he was smart, sometimes infuriatingly so, but he was also very much a hands-on kind of man, more at home in the corral than sitting behind a desk. He could certainly negotiate a deal and did his fair share of admin work for the ranch, but being out with the horses and cattle was where he was the happiest. Not that she wanted to think about Mitch being happy. She didn't care one iota. Caring would mean feeling, and she had experienced enough feelings to do with Mitch to last her a lifetime. All she wanted was for them to be able to be parents in a way that was best for their child.

"Does Grant visit regularly?" she enquired, remembering his youngest brother fondly. It had been challenging for him when his teacher also became his sister-in-law, but Grant was good-natured and likable and got along with most people.

"Every couple of weeks," Mitch replied. "He's busy with his new job. Ellie has seen him more than I do in the last couple of years, since she was doing a course at the technical college in Rapid City and would spend a couple of nights at Grant's apartment when she had to be there for classes. She's doing her last few semesters online, so she can be more hands on at the ranch. You know Ellie—horses are in her DNA."

"She's had a good role model," Tess remarked, and meant it. The truth was, Mitch has been an amazing guardian to his siblings for the last sixteen years and deserved the acknowledgment. Plus, she knew it meant he would be an amazing father to their child. Suddenly she was compelled to ask him the question that had been churning inside her for the last twenty-four hours. "Are you really happy about the baby, Mitch?"

"Yes," he said quietly. "Honestly, after everything that happened between us, Tess, I'm delighted that we can share this little miracle."

"You don't regret not going ahead with the vasectomy?"

He sighed heavily. "I don't think I would have done it," he said, and glanced at her. "I only said it to…to…"

"To control the situation?" she said when his words trailed.

"I know it probably seemed that way at the time. But honestly, I think I'd hoped it would somehow help you heal," he said softly. "You were hurting. I didn't know what to say or do. And we were so far apart… I don't know… Maybe I thought an ultimatum would bring you back to me. In hindsight, it was a reckless thing to say and if I had known what the consequence would be, I like to think I would have done things differently."

"That's not what you said yesterday," she reminded him.

"Yesterday I was in shock," he said candidly. "The last person I expected to turn up at my door was you. After what happened in Sioux Falls, I believed we were done for good. You left so quickly I didn't have a chance to process what it meant."

"I didn't think I would get pregnant," she said, hearing a veiled accusation in his tone. She knew Mitch was peeved by the way she had practically bolted from his hotel room all those months ago. "And I didn't want a postmortem. You know very well that I don't do that casually and—"

"Neither do I," he added quickly, cutting her off.

"I haven't been with anyone since we separated," she admitted, and then wished she hadn't, because she didn't want him reading too much into what her behavior meant. "Can you say the same thing?"

"Would it matter?" he fired back.

"You're a free agent," she said, wishing they would hurry and reach their destination soon. "You can do what you like."

"I haven't been engraving notches on my bedpost, if that's what you're inferring."

She shrugged as heat crawled up her neck. "I'm not interested in—"

"You seem interested," he said. "But I wasn't a player before you, or after you, Tess. Like you, I prefer sex to mean something. Even if, at the time, I thought it was simply goodbye."

She swallowed the sudden burning in her throat. To be reminded of their time in Sioux Falls was painful. Because he obviously had believed it would be the last time they would be together…like a catharsis…a way of purging her from his system. But for Tess—she had been abruptly dragged back into her safe place, to his arms, to the memory of all they had once been to one another.

Thankfully, they had arrived at the Triple C and Tess took the chance to change the subject again.

"So, you'll get to keep Dolly's colt?"

"Yes," he replied. "That was the deal. The ranch needs a new stallion and Alvarez will get the initial option on the first of this colt's progeny."

"Ellie doesn't like him," she remarked as they drove up the driveway.

"Ramon Alvarez is a tough businessman, and he's not the easiest guy to get along with. But this deal will be good for Triple C. You know there are half a dozen ranches offering exactly what we offer here, but with Volcán's proven bloodline, we can be a step ahead of the competition. He's a champion reining horse and his offspring sell for big money."

"Is the ranch in financial trouble?" she asked.

"No," he replied as they pulled up outside the house. "But over the last few years I've watched as several spreads in the area went under or have been sold off. I won't allow that for the Triple C. This place belongs to my family and now to my child," he said, and glanced at her stomach. "I'll do whatever I have to do to keep it safe."

Tess nodded. Whatever Mitch's faults, he had an unwavering loyalty to his home and family. She opened the door, and Mitch was out of the vehicle within seconds and around the passenger side to help her out.

Once they were inside, she followed him up the stairs, taking a moment to reacquaint herself with the wall of photographs. She'd never met Mitch's parents, but had heard countless stories about his grandparents, Henry and Aurora Culhane. Of course, she knew the whole story about Billie-Jack. All the memories, all the tragedy that the Culhanes had endured had somehow made them stronger and more resilient, and she admired them for their ability to push past the challenges and get on with things. Like Hank had, enduring countless surgeries after the accident and still becoming one of the nicest and most generous people she had ever known. Or Joss, who was raising his young daughters alone since his wife's death. Or Ellie—losing her mother and being left by her father—and still finding a way to become a strong and fiercely independent women with her brother's guidance.

"I thought this room would make the best nursery," Mitch said when she reached the top of the stairs. He pointed to the second door on the left. "Grant's old room. A coat of paint and some baby furniture and I think it will do the job."

Tess didn't dare look in the direction of the master suite. It was the room they'd shared as husband and wife. The room where they'd whispered words of love countless times. The room where she'd told him she was leaving the ranch—and him—for good.

"I'm sure the room will be fine," she said, and hovered in the doorway. The room was empty, except for a bed, dresser and chair in the corner. The posters and trophies adorning the walls and shelves were now gone. No doubt stored away alongside the belongings from Jake, Joss and Hank's old rooms.

Mitch was now in the room, looking around. "We could drive into Rapid City and go shopping. You know, pick up a cradle and changing table and baby monitor and things like that."

Tess looked at him. He was, she had to admit, trying to keep the communication between them open and civil. Only, she knew he had an endgame. Still, if she disagreed, it would just create more drama between them and that was the last thing she wanted.

"Sure," she said agreeably. "I did mention I had an ultrasound appointment next week, so we could go shopping that day."

"Sounds like a plan," he said, and grinned. "Now, how about lunch?"

Tess glanced at her watch and saw that it was after one o'clock. "I'm not hungry," she fibbed, ignoring the way her tummy rumbled at the mention of food.

"Sure you are," he said, and ushered her forward. "You hardly touched your pancakes this morning. It's Mrs. Bailey's day off, but I'm sure I can rustle up something in the kitchen."

A minute later they were down the stairs and in the kitchen. Tess moved around one side of the counter and watched as Mitch pulled things from the refrigerator. He looked very at ease in the kitchen. Then again he looked at ease anywhere. It was one of his qualities—the ability to appear right at home doing anything at all. Like when he was in the corral working one of the horses, or helping out his brother with babysitting, or bent over the engine of a truck, or out in the dead of winter searching for a lost tourist with Shanook at his side. Or in the bedroom, she thought and then pushed the thought from her head. Remembering the kind of lover he was was too dumb for words.

"Ham and cheese okay?" he asked.

Tess nodded and moved around the counter. "I can help."

"Don't trust my cooking?"

"Making a sandwich isn't exactly cooking," she said. She pulled bread from its wrapper, buttered the bread and waited for him to pass her the fillings. "Will Ellie be joining us?"

"I doubt it," he replied, and grabbed plates and a knife. "She usually hangs out with Winona on Saturdays."

Tess remembered Winona, Ellie's closest friend, fondly. Winona was the only grandchild of the previous foreman at the Triple C, Red Sheehan, and as kids the girls had been inseparable.

"Ellie told me about Red's strokes," she said, recalling a conversation she'd had with his sister the day before, while Mitch had been dealing with Dolly's foal. "She said Red still lives at the ranch."

Mitch nodded. "He's paralyzed down his left side, but still helps out around the place when he can. He'll always have a home here."

Of course, she would expect nothing less from Mitch. "Does Win still live with her grandfather in one of the cottages?" she asked.

Mitch shook his head. "Nah…she moved into town a few years ago. She works at the tourist center when she's not helping out here. She's a good kid. Red raised her right after her mom died."

"I'm sure living on the ranch helped," Tess said, and smiled.

"I hope so. I'd like to think it's a good place to raise a family. I guess we'll find out soon enough."

Mitch grabbed a couple of sodas from the refrigerator, and once Tess had piled the sandwiches on a plate, they moved around the countertop and sat side by side at the island.

"I was thinking about names," she said, and picked the crust off her sandwich. "I mean, for the baby."

He met her gaze and then swiped the unwanted crust off her plate. It had been a thing they'd always done... Mitch ate her crusts, she ate his garnish. Funny, she thought, how some things came back as easily as breathing.

"Any preferences?" he asked.

"Charlie," she said. "Which could work for a boy or a girl, after your great-grandfather. Or Jacob, after your brother if it's a boy."

"Alexander or Alexandria," he said. "After your dad."

Tess's throat tightened. She was only six when her father died, but she remembered the pain of losing him like it was yesterday. She was touched that Mitch would suggest honoring her dad by naming their child after him. Although she loved her stepdad, some days she missed her father more than words could say. "Thank you, I'd like that."

"So, Charlie Alexander, or Charlotte Alexandria, it is."

"Charlie Alexander Culhane," she said, and nodded. "Has a nice sound to it."

He smiled. "You're convinced it's a boy?"

She nodded. "Mother's intuition. I'm sure he'll be a great kid."

"With you as his mom, he's got it in the bag."

Tess felt something flutter deep in her chest. Being with Mitch was becoming way too easy. And way too complicated. And suddenly the enormity of what they were heading to—the child they would be sharing—struck her with the force of a freight train. She swallowed hard and blinked back the heat burning behind her eyes.

"Mitch… I…"

He reached out and grasped her hand, linking their fingers tightly together. The intimacy of the gesture was profound and she let the tears fall, unable to hold back the tide of emotion. Things had changed so much since that afternoon in Sioux Falls. Tess knew there was no going back to how things had been—to her steady and predicable life, to her teaching job, her small circle of friends, her everyday existence that suddenly seemed like exactly that. Just existing. Simply getting up every morning and going through the motions of her life. Without Mitch. Without memory. Without any sense of joy and any real hope for a happy future. Looking back to how she'd been prior to that afternoon in Sioux Falls, Tess knew she had been playacting at her own life.

With his other hand, he rubbed at her cheek, tenderly, wiping away the tears. "I know it's hard for you, Tess," he said. "I know you're confused and still mad at me and probably want to run a mile right now. But we can get through this…together."

It sounded so simple, and yet Tess knew it was impossible.

The deep intimacy of the moment was acute and she rested her cheek against his palm, finding solace and comfort in his touch even though she knew she was crazy for letting herself be vulnerable to him…and to their complicated history.

Because it would never truly be history…particularly since they now shared a child.

Mitch fought the urge to fold her into his arms and kiss her. She looked so lost, so achingly vulnerable. He hated that he was responsible for some of that. With their past it was impossible for feelings to stay tamped down and out of sight. And, frankly, he didn't want that. If they had any hope of getting back together, of making a life as a real family for the sake of their child, then he had to let go of his bitterness and resentment toward her for running out on him so many years ago.

He brought one of her hands to his mouth and kissed her knuckles, lingering for a moment to inhale the scent of the lotion she used, because it kicked at a memory and took him back ten years. It was the same rose fragrance, her signature scent, he used to call it. Old-fashioned, he used to tease her, and yet undeniably sexy. Without a word, Mitch drew her closer, his hand cradling her face for a moment before moving around to her nape.

"Don't be afraid to remember, Tes," he said, inviting her forward until her face was directly in front of his. "Or to feel."

Her eyes glistened, her mouth parted fractionally, and her cheeks were flushed with color. And he was lost. He kissed her, claiming her lips gently, waiting for her resistance, and when he found none, he went a little further, deepening the kiss. She moaned low in her throat and her hand came to rest on his bicep, holding firm. Her lips accepted his, and he gently wound his tongue around hers, going in deeper, softer. Then he pulled back a little, remembering how she liked to be kissed, feeling his whole body tighten and respond at the seductive dance. In all his life, no other kiss had both tortured and moved him simultaneously. Only Tess, and the sweet taste of her mouth and the soft, erotic slide of her tongue against his.

"Oh…sorry, guys!"

Ellie, in all her loud and surprised glory, had bounded unexpectedly into the room and was staring at them with a delighted expression. Tess pulled away immediately and slid off the stool. Mitch did the same seconds later, and they both faced his sister as she moved into the room.

"Sorry," Ellie said again, and grinned. "I didn't mean to interrupt you while you were eating."

The double meaning of her words was blatantly obvious, and Mitch watched as Tess colored hotly. There was, he realized, still something elementally innocent about his ex-wife. She possessed a quiet sort of modesty, almost shyness, which he'd recognized the first time they'd met. He remembered how he hadn't summoned the courage to kiss her on their first date, fearful that she'd balk and run. They'd been dating a couple of months before they'd made love, even though he was head over heels in love with her by then.

And I still am…

Mitch shook off the feeling, pushing good sense back into his brain. Getting Tess back for the sake of their child was one thing; falling back in love with her another altogether. Love complicated everything. And since losing her had ripped his heart out, he definitely didn't want to go back for another round of that. But he wanted her back, no doubt about it. He wanted their family to be together. He would make it happen—he merely had to find the right angle to get her to agree.

Ellie marched into the room and hugged Tess affectionately. There had never been any doubt how much Tess cared for his family, Ellie and Grant in particular.

It could be worked to his advantage, he figured, to help Tess remember all they had once had.

"It's so good to see you again," Ellie said cheerfully. "I was going to call Annie today and start making plans for the baby shower. Although," she said, "maybe we will be having a bridal shower first?"

Mitch's brows came together and he shook his head toward his sister. As much as he adored Ellie, diplomacy and discretion were not part of her makeup. "I've scheduled a conference call with Alvarez this afternoon," he reminded her to change the subject. "Five o'clock. We need to discuss the next round of insemination, too."

Ellie shrugged, clearly not in the mood for shoptalk when she could have *baby talk* with her adored former sister-in-law. Mitch had the thought that perhaps allowing them to spend time together might work to his advantage.

"Be back soon," he said to Tess, and grabbed his hat off the peg by the door. "I need to catch up with Wes. I'll take you back to Annie's once I'm done."

He left without another word and headed directly for the stables. Wes was in the office, on the computer and placing a feed order, and Mitch spent half an hour with the other man going over the branding schedule for the next month and several other things that needed to be done the following week. Afterward, he checked on Dolly's colt and was happy to see the youngster was suckling and moving around the stall on gangly legs.

Mitch grabbed some hay and stuffed it into the net. He smiled as Dolly gently pushed the foal aside to get to her feed. She was a good mom, firm but affectionate, and the colt was clearly thriving. Relief pitched in his chest and he sighed. It had been a long couple of years getting the Alvarez deal to this point, and he was pleased it was over and that the foal was doing so well. The last thing he needed was distraction when he had more important things to think about.

Like getting Tess to come home.

"How's he doing?"

Her voice made him turn instantly. She was standing about five feet away, arms crossed. She didn't look particularly happy with him and clearly had something on her mind. Like their kiss, he suspected. "He's great. You know, we still haven't named him. The offer is still there if you'd like to pick something."

She stepped closer and peered over the stall, tugging at her bottom lip with her teeth. "Monty," she said after a moment.

Mitch nodded. "Monty it is. Tess," he said, and took a breath. "If you—"

"What happened in Sioux Falls," she said tightly. "That's not going to happen again. If that's what you're thinking."

"I'm not thinking anything," he replied, and bolted the stall door.

"Then why did you kiss me?"

"Why did you kiss me back?" Mitch asked. He propped his hands on his hips. "Frankly, Tess, kissing you comes as naturally to me as breathing. I would think you'd know that by now."

She stared at him, her eyes wide. "I know that you—"

"It was just a kiss, Tess, stop overanalyzing it." He grinned, knowing his casual tone would infuriate her, when inside he ached to kiss her again.

"You're such a jerk, Mitch."

"Part of my charm," he quipped. "Did you have a nice chat with Ellie? She really cares about you, you know. I know she's over the moon that you're back. I mean, not back at the ranch, of *course*, but back in town. And she's really excited about the baby."

One brow angled. "Clever. I love how you think you can defuse my temper by mentioning your family."

"Oh, you're having a temper tantrum?" he queried.

She glared at him, looking like she wanted to take a swing for a second, and then laughed. "Can you take me home?"

"Sure, I can take you back to Annie's," he said pointedly, refusing to call the McCall ranch her home.

She waited a few minutes while he went back inside to get his keys and jacket. They barely spoke during the trip and once they were back at his cousin's ranch she was clearly eager to go inside.

"I'll see you for my doctor's appointment on Thursday, if you still want to—"

"I'll pick you up," he said quickly, and grabbed a business card from the console. "That's my cell, send me a text with the time you want me here."

She nodded and took the card. "Okay, see you then."

He waited until she was well up the path before driving off, and was by the gate when he pulled out his cell and made a call. His brother answered on the third ring.

"I need a favor," he said.

"What kind of favor?"

"One with plausible deniability," he said, and told his brother exactly what he wanted.

The Triple C was his home. And Tess's. It should be their child's home, too.

And all he had to do was convince her that they belonged together.

Until then, he had to think of a way to keep her close.

It wasn't about control, even though he knew she'd accuse him of thinking that way; it was about making sure she was safe…that their baby was safe. And if she was determined to live alone, then Mitch was equally determined to have some say in where…even if she didn't know it.

Chapter Six

"So, are you ready to *really* talk?"

On Tuesday morning, after a couple of days of locking herself inside Annie's small house on the McCall ranch like a hibernating polar bear, Tess met her sister in the kitchen and accepted the enquiry she knew was inevitable.

"I'm ready."

"What's going on, Tess? What are you not telling me?"

"Mitch wants to get remarried."

Annie's eyes bulged. "Wow. And is that what you want?"

"Of course not," she replied. "Mitch and I are divorced. And the reason we divorced still exists."

Annie's expression softened. "It was a long time ago, Tess. And since you're now pregnant, he obviously didn't have a—"

"The hurt is still there." She pressed a hand to her chest. "The betrayal. When I had the last miscarriage, he wanted to be in control of the situation and all I wanted was for him to hold me and say it would be okay, that we'd try again. But he wouldn't have it. He wouldn't see past his determination to have everything go his own way. Whatever we had, it's over. All I want to do now is make a home for my child."

"Without Mitch?"

"*With* Mitch having as much access to our child as he wants to have."

"What if he doesn't agree to your terms, Tess? Have you thought about that?"

"Do you mean have I considered the idea of him going for shared custody? Well, I hadn't," she admitted. "Until he mentioned it. If he does, I'll deal with that when it happens."

"Perhaps you should get a lawyer," Annie suggested. "I'm pretty sure that the best lawyer in town is one the Culhanes frequently use. I know David does. But maybe there's someone else who could help you."

"Maybe," she said. "I'll let you know. So," she said, swiftly shifting the subject. "What's happening with you?"

Her stepsister shrugged. "Nothing's changed. I've been thinking about leaving my job, as you've probably worked out."

"Does David know that?"

Annie shook her head. "The truth is, I'm still undecided."

"The kids will miss you."

"I know," her sister said, sighing heavily. "But I can't work as a nanny forever."

"And your pen pal?"

Annie had been corresponding with a man in Colorado for a couple of months. She didn't know how serious it was, but she was happy that her sister was thinking about her own future—even if it meant leaving David's employ.

"We email," Annie corrected. "And since I've never met him, we're simply friends."

"You might," Tess suggested, "if you take a much-deserved and needed vacation. I hear the Rockies are amazing at this time of year."

"Don't think talking about my complicated life is going to distract me from being concerned about you," Annie said evenly. "I know you, Tess. I can tell that being back here is bringing back a whole lot of memories. And I don't want to seem like I'm being neutral on the subject because you know that I support you one hundred percent," she said, and then took a breath. "But maybe Mitch has a point?"

Tess's gaze narrowed. "You think I should marry him?"

"I think you should do what makes you happy," her sister said. "And Mitch did make you happy…once."

"Past tense," she said. "I believe marriage should be about love, not because Mitch thinks it's the right thing to do. I want my baby to have a father who is present in his life, but I don't want him present in mine."

As she said the words, an inexplicable pain pierced her chest. But she had to say it out loud, had to live and breathe it and make it real to herself. She wasn't about to get reeled back into Mitch's vortex, despite how good the kiss had been. *The kiss.* Which had pretty much been all she'd thought about for the past couple of days. That, and the fact that her ex-husband had been conspicuously absent. She'd expected him to turn up on her doorstep every day so they could rehash the same old argument about her returning to the ranch. However, to his credit, he'd kept his promise and had merely responded to her text message about collecting her on Thursday for her doctor's appointment. But rather than put her at ease, his lack of communication only amplified her anxiety and put her on edge.

"I can't imagine Mitch taking a back seat, can you?" Annie asked.

Tess shrugged again. Her sister was right. As much as he appeared to be a relaxed and even-tempered cowboy, a man of the land who was happier in denim and a Stetson, there was an element of the pure alpha male about him. Perhaps because he'd been thrust into manhood at such an early age and had to take up the reins as the head of his family. But she suspected that there had always been something *in charge* about Mitch, even from infancy.

"No," she admitted. "I can't. I'm sure he's trying to work out every angle he possibly can to get me to agree to move back into the ranch."

"Well," Annie said with a grin, "running that big house always did look good on you."

Tess wasn't about to disagree. She'd loved being on the Triple C. She'd adored the big kitchen and the wide staircase, and the large master bedroom suite with its view of the entire ranch. The bedroom she'd shared with her husband. Where they'd loved, laughed and lost. In the end, it was where she'd told him she was leaving, where she'd packed her bags and walked out from his life and their marriage. The memory made her shiver, and she wrapped her arms around herself, resting her hands on her belly.

"I have to get back to work," Annie said as she grabbed her coat. "I promised Jasper I'd have his Halloween costume finished tonight and I have eight arachnid legs to stuff and sew."

"Halloween is still a couple of weeks away," she said.

"Are getting in early with the costumes in case you *do* decide to leave?"

Annie grinned. "Jasper likes to be organized. Chances are he might change his mind and want to trick or treat as a storm trooper, so I may need to improvise."

Tess smiled warmly, thinking how her sister was so generous and kind and how much she adored David McCall's kids. Too bad the stupid man had all the awareness and sensitivity of a rock. Otherwise, he would realize what a treasure Annie was and stop treating her like an employee.

"I hope I'm half the mom that you are," Tess said gently and hugged her sister. "I know you're worried about me, but I promise I'm fine. Once I find a place to live and get settled, things will get back to normal and I won't feel as though I'm living my life from one improvisation to the next."

Annie hugged her in return, and once her sister left, Tess spent the remainder of the day doing a little light housework and reading. Early on Wednesday afternoon, she headed into Cedar River and dropped by the real estate office, hopeful she could check out a few more listings. There were several that interested her, and Leola showed her two possible places.

The first one was way too large, but the second place was better than expected. The house was a three-bedroom brick and tile, with a good-sized, fully fenced yard and an overgrown vegetable garden out the back. When they returned to the real estate office around two, the agent handed her a contract and Tess said she'd think about it overnight.

Since she'd parked in an hour zone, Tess took a walk down Main Street and made her way into the boutique beside the beauty parlor. She tried a few things and settled on a new pair of maternity jeans and a knitted poncho she figured would fit over her expanding belly in the next few months. She impulsively added a cherry-red sweater that caught her eye, a trio of assorted pink scrunchies and a dark cashmere scarf. Once she'd paid the clerk and had her parcels, Tess left the shop and walked back into the street.

Unexpectedly she came face-to-face with her former brother-in-law Joss and his two daughters, eleven-year-old Sissy and eight-year-old Clare. The girls were shy at first, until Joss explained who she was, and how she was having a baby who would be their cousin. Then she was hugged, and Clare began tugging at her shopping bags enquiring about what was inside. Tess took out the scrunchies and handed one to each of the girls, and they both hugged her again.

Clare pulled on her father's arm. "Can Tess come to my birthday party, Daddy?"

He grinned. "Of course," he replied, and looked at Tess. "Saturday, twelve o'clock at the ranch. There'll be cake and party games. David's kids are coming, so your sister will probably be there, too, if that's helpful."

And Mitch will be there.

"I'd love to," she said, and nodded toward a smiling Clare. "Thank you for inviting me."

"No worries," he said. "So, my brother said you were looking for a house?"

A seed of suspicion sprouted. "That's right."

"You know, the elderly lady a couple of doors down from us recently moved into a nursing home. She's Mrs. B's mother-in-law," he added. "Well, anyhow, after old Mrs. Bailey left, I bought the house and was planning on leasing it out. If you're interested I could—"

"Is this offer your brother's idea?"

Joss, who was about as honest as the day was long, simply shrugged. "We thought it would—"

"We?" she asked, cutting him off.

"He's just trying to—"

"I know exactly what he's trying to do. Control everything, as usual," she said, her quiet tone defying the irritation coursing through her blood. "I'll see you Saturday." She gave the girls another quick hug before she headed to her car. Once she was back at the Annie's, Tess unloaded her parcels, stomped around the house for half an hour and then grabbed her bag and car keys and headed straight for the Triple C.

Mitch was hauling bales of hay with one of the ranch hands when he spotted Tess striding through the feed shed, arms crossed, her mouth set in a tight line. Still, in dark jeans, glittery flats, a red smock and woolen coat, she looked so beautiful that his heart felt as though it literally skipped a beat. Her blond hair was down, and her cheeks were flushed, as though she'd been working herself up into a kind of temper tantrum.

Joss had called him, of course, and explained how his idea of offering Tess the house had been received like a lead weight. It didn't look as though her mood had improved in the hour and a half since his brother's call.

"Ah, Roy," he said to the young ranch hand. "Take a break, will you?"

The younger man noticed Tess and quickly dropped the hay and made his way out through the side door. Mitch remained where he was, about ten feet up, standing on a stack of bales.

"I want to talk to you," she said, her chest heaving. "Now."

Mitch jumped down and met her in the center of the shed. "What's up?"

"I'm not going to live next door to your brother so that you can get him to keep an eye on me," she said quickly. "If that's what you were thinking."

He shrugged. "It's a nice house on a nice street. And actually, it's not next door. It's a couple of houses away. I think your old friend Lucy Monero lives next door. Isn't she part of the reason you want to have the baby at the community hospital, since she's a doctor on staff there? She married Brant Parker a couple of years ago. I think they've got a toddler, although I'm not sure if it's a boy or a girl. Does knowing that make you less suspicious of my motives?"

She frowned. "I thought… I thought…"

"The worst of me," he said quietly. "As usual."

She harrumphed. "Joss made the offer and I assumed you—"

"Were trying to be the all-seeing, all-knowing, all-controlling pain-in-the-neck who wants to tell you what to do. I get it. You're still angry with me and you don't trust me. I can read you, Tess. I know you're doing your utmost to hang on to your resentment. Well, it goes both ways. I've got a fair bit of resentment myself for the way you walked out on me and on *us* four years ago. But I'm trying to get past it for the sake of our child."

It was a nice speech. One aimed directly at the core of the problems between them.

She resented him. He resented her. The problem was that it had taken Mitch about twenty-four hours of her being back in Cedar River to realize that despite everything, he *still* had feelings for her, and it was very clear that Tess had moved on from loving him a long time ago. Which of course made him resent her even more, because knowing it battered his pride and made him also feel like the biggest fool of all time.

"Okay," she said after a moment, her expression softening a little. "I'll look at the house."

"I think that's the most sensible thing you've said since Friday."

She smiled humorlessly. "Do you do that simply to make me crazy, or what?"

"Probably. We can look at the place tomorrow, on the way back from the doctor's appointment."

"And if I said I don't need you to accompany me, would it make any difference?"

"I know where Joss keeps the spare key," he said. "Now, what time tomorrow?"

She muttered something about nine thirty in the morning, giving them time to make the appointment and allow for any delays, and then turned on her heels and left. Mitch stayed where he was for a while, propped against a hay bale, trying to make sense of what had happened to his life in the past five days. He'd deliberately left her alone since Saturday sensing she needed space and knowing she would wrap a cloak of resistance around herself if he pushed the issue about moving back to the ranch. Small steps were what he needed. Mitch pushed himself off the hay bale, stretched out his shoulders and got back to work, figuring it was what he needed to keep his mind clear.

He slept poorly that night and woke up around seven with a crick in his neck. He showered, changed and ate the toast Mrs. B passed him when he entered the kitchen for coffee. He had an eight-o'clock meeting with Wes and Ellie and left for the McCall ranch at ten past nine. Tess was waiting out in front of Annie's small house when he arrived and he got out quickly to open the passenger door.

He didn't say she looked nice, even though she did, because he figured she wouldn't welcome his compliments.

She said hello and that was all, and they were through the front gates before she spoke again, giving him the address of the obstetrician in Rapid City.

"Will this be your last ultrasound before the baby's born?" Mitch asked as they headed onto the road.

"Probably not," she replied. "Since I'm considered high risk because of my history, my doctor in Sioux Falls wants to make sure everything is okay as I go from one trimester to the next. My blood pressure is monitored weekly and I make sure I report any changes."

Mitch's stomach tightened. "Changes?"

"Like spotting or cramping."

"Have you experienced any of those things?" he asked quietly.

"Not so far," she said, knowing exactly what he was asking without hearing the words. "Somehow, this time, I feel different. Stronger. It's like I just *know* everything will be okay. That might sound foolish, but I can't describe it any other way."

It didn't sound foolish. It sounded exactly like what he would expect her to feel. Long ago, when she'd endured loss, she'd grieved every miscarriage so profoundly he'd experienced an acute sense of helplessness that wounded him right to the soul. Every time she'd fallen pregnant, at first she was joyful, then hopeful, and then, once she realized the baby was unable to cling to her womb, she had possessed a look that had haunted him—a look of inconsolable anguish.

What she didn't need, he realized, was stress of any kind.

"I'm sorry if I overstepped with the house thing," he said with a heavy sigh. "I want you to be safe and figured that if you live a couple of doors down from my brother you'll always have someone looking out for you. Stupidly macho, I know, but I can't help it."

"You mean, you can't help who you are?" she suggested. "I get that, Mitch. I know you've spent your adult life being the glue that keeps your family together. And despite how it seems, I do appreciate your concern. But I have a hard time dealing with the way you're overreaching, and I don't like feeling smothered, okay? Look, I'm back because I want our child to have a relationship with you. Because I know you'll be a good father to him."

And that's all.

"Is there someone else?" he asked, thinking about the possibility for the first time in any real sense.

"What?"

"Do you have someone, you know, a man you're seeing or something, and is that why you won't—"

"I see. The only reason I might be foolish enough to *not* come running back to you and the ranch is because I'm seeing someone?" she asked, cutting him off. "Really? Is your ego that healthy that you can't imagine I might simply *not* be interested in picking up where we left off?"

"It occurred to me that you might have met someone," he said, ignoring the dig about his inflated ego.

"No," she said. "I told you already I'm single. And I'm not interested in meeting anyone."

"But you might?" he asked, hating how the idea of her being with someone else, *loving* someone else, cut him through to the core. "And if he's to be a stepdad to my child, then it involves us both."

"If I do fall in love, you'll be the first to know," she assured him, and he noticed she was grinning a fraction, as though she was amused by his words. "By the way,

I've been invited to Clare's birthday party on Saturday. Is there anything I can do to help with the organizing?"

"Ask Ellie, she's the party planner. Which reminds me, she's badgering me about arranging a baby shower for you, so if you can let her know when and where she can start making plans, that would be great."

They talked the remainder of the way about his sister and the Alvarez deal, and she asked questions about the ranch and nothing more was said about *their* relationship. Or lack thereof.

Rapid City was a busy town, and it took a few minutes to get a parking spot outside the suite of professional medical offices. But once they were inside and were greeted by reception, they were shown into an examination room within minutes and a nurse arrived to help Tess prepare for the test. They'd been through the process before, so Mitch knew he had little to do until the technician arrived. Tess lay on the bed, her belly modestly exposed, as the technician spread gel over her skin. Another woman came into the room and introduced herself as Dr. Huang, and soon the procedure was underway. Mitch sat by Tess's shoulder, watching the monitor as the doctor ran the ultrasound across her stomach. It didn't take long to see the shape of their child on the screen and he blinked back the heat burning behind his eyes as their baby's image came to life. It was a profoundly intimate moment and one he would cherish for the remainder of his life.

Mitch didn't realize he'd grasped Tess's hand until he felt her fingers tighten around his. He glanced at her face and saw her eyes were glistening with tears. And rightly so. It took all his strength to hold back his own.

"Well, everything looks fine," the doctor assured them and smiled. "Would you like to know the baby's sex?"

Tess looked at him and nodded. "Yes, I think it's time we found out."

Mitch's throat burned and he nodded agreeably.

The doctor smiled at them in turn. "You have a son."

He blinked again as Tess's grip tightened and she let out a long and shuddering sigh. "Told you so," she said softly, as tears fell across her cheeks.

Mitch reached out and gently wiped the moisture away with his thumb, thinking he'd never seen her look more beautiful than she did in that moment.

"He's growing exactly how he should be," the doctor said, "and with a very strong heartbeat. Would you like a photo to take with you today?"

Mitch nodded, his throat so tight he couldn't speak.

It was Tess who said what he couldn't. "That would be wonderful. Two copies please."

Two copies. Because most couples would share the joy of their child together. Most couples weren't so emotionally far apart. He hated how it made him feel…included in the moment, but excluded in their future.

The technician and doctor left the room, and Tess grabbed a handful of tissues from the table by the bed and began wiping the gel off her belly. Mitch made a move to help her and she stilled instantly, holding up her hand.

"I've got it," she said, and grabbed some more tissues.

He watched as she struggled and then took the tissues from her hand. "You missed a spot," he said, and wiped the gel away from her left hip. "Stop being so damned independent for a moment and let me help."

She rolled her eyes and flopped her hands to her sides. "Fine. You don't have to get so heated up about it. Go ahead."

He cleaned her up as quickly as he could and tossed the tissues into the trash can by the door, trying to ignore the flicker of awareness rumbling through his system. "See, I touched you and the world didn't end."

"You know very well that I've never complained about you touching me," she shot back. "That's one thing we always seemed to get right."

He chuckled. "I guess so. Chemistry, huh?"

"Sex," she corrected, tugging her smock over her belly. "But I'm not going to lose my senses again, Mitch."

He laughed softly. "Your senses? Is that what happened in Sioux Falls?"

"Yes," she admitted. "I was caught up in memory and seeing you again brought it all back. At first, the good… and then…"

"The bad?" he finished for her. "That's why you left as though your feet were on fire."

"I didn't think there was any point hanging around in case things got awkward. Silly, I suppose." She shook her head. "We should have talked. Said goodbye. Something."

The doctor returned before he could reply, but he was struck by the regret in her voice.

With the pictures of their son safely stored in separate envelopes, Tess took a few minutes to get dressed. After a brief consultation with the doctor about the next couple of months and what they should expect with the pregnancy, including booking in their next prenatal appointment, they headed back outside. It was cool out and he noticed that she shivered. He immediately shrugged out of his coat and draped it around her shoulders.

"You'll catch pneumonia," she said, and tried to brush off his intentions.

"No, I won't," he assured her as they walked toward the truck. "And I wouldn't care if I did. You and the baby come first, understand?"

She stopped walking and stared up at him, her hand

suddenly coming out to grasp his arm. She swallowed hard, her lovely face filled with emotion that had very little to do with him and everything to do with baby hormones and the fact they'd just witnessed their son resting peacefully within her womb.

"Tess?"

Her eyes glistened. "We're having a baby," she said, and shuddered. "We're really having a baby. No one knows how much I want this more than you, Mitch. And I'm glad, after all the babies we lost, that we'll get to share."

"Me, too," he said, and covered her hand with his.

"And I... I..."

There were tears on her cheeks and he wiped them with his thumb, suddenly filled with the idea that he wanted to kiss her and hold her and make everything right in the world for the only woman who had ever had his heart.

"You, what?"

She half smiled. "I'm hungry," she said, and hiccuped.

Mitch laughed. "Okay." He ushered her into the truck. "What would you like?"

"Hot dog," she replied. "With mayonnaise *and* pickles."

He screwed his face up. "Gross. But I'll get you what you want."

Once they were back on the road they found a diner, and bought hot dogs and sodas that they ate in the truck. He drove directly to Mustang Street and pulled up outside the house one door down from his brother's home.

"This is nice," she said as she got out.

"Yeah, Joss bought the place a couple of months ago. He's got quite a portfolio," he said and grinned. "My brother the real estate magnate."

"You must be proud of the way all your siblings have turned out."

"I am," he replied. "They're good people."

"Because of you," she added. "You're the reason why. You kept your family together, when so many others would have given up and only considered themselves."

"It was the right thing to do."

She touched his arm. "I've always admired that about you."

Mitch looked to where her hand lay and felt the warmth from her touch. "I don't always get it right though."

She smiled and removed her hand. "Does anyone?"

The small home was well maintained, with a generous garden and fenced all the way around. There was a porch and a swing and French-styled shutters along the front.

"Do you want to check it out?" he asked.

She nodded and walked up the path and through the gate. Mitch found the hidden key under a rock by the steps and opened the front door. The scent of cedar floor polish was unmistakable, and her heels clicked over the floorboards as she wandered down the hallway and into the front living room.

"It's lovely," she said, and turned to face him.

They were close, barely a foot apart, and it was impossible to ignore the intimacy that had been building all morning. Mitch reached out and touched her cheek, stroking her jawline, curling his hand around her nape and gently urging her forward. She took a step and looked up at him, smiling in a way that made his heart beat like a jackhammer in his chest.

"Do you think you could be happy here?" he asked softly.

She nodded. "I'm happy right now."

His thundering heart raced faster. "Tess…about what I said earlier…about you finding someone. I don't think… I don't think I could bear it."

Her hand came up and curled around his shoulder. "I know that."

She moved closer and rested her head against his chest. Mitch wound his arms around her, pulling her close, feeling her lovely curves. With their baby between them, he had no words to articulate the jumble of emotions running through his head. The intimacy and closeness was profound and suddenly overwhelming, and he knew exactly what he wanted.

"Will you come back to me?" he breathed the words into her hair. "Please."

She stiffened, but didn't pull away. "I can't."

He knew she'd say it, and the words made him ache deep down. "You're scared?"

She nodded. "Aren't you?"

"Of needing you again? Of loving you again?" He sucked in a hard and shuddering breath. "Terrified. But I'm willing to risk it for the sake of our son."

She pulled back, untangling herself from his arms. "You're braver than me. But I'll consider living in this house so your brother can watch over me from a distance."

"Thank you," he said and smiled. "Would you like to go shopping now?"

She considered it and shook her head. "Not today. Next time, okay?"

"Sure," he replied, thinking he'd had a small win by her agreement to live in Joss's house. But it wasn't enough. It would never be enough. He wanted her back. In his house. In his bed. But he couldn't push her. Couldn't demand. Couldn't fall to her feet and beg her to reconsider. That would be too humiliating.

It was after two when they arrived back at the McCall ranch. He spotted his cousin's silver Mercedes SUV in the driveway. David was the most urban rancher he knew. In fact, he wasn't much of rancher at all and all the cattle on the place belonged to Mitch, but he was happy to lease the grazing land. David was happier behind a desk, although he *was* handy on a horse. They'd been best friends as well as cousins for all of their lives and he knew the other man wouldn't mind Tess staying at the ranch for as long as she needed. But Tess was independent and wanted to do things her own way.

"Your cousin's home early," she remarked as they pulled up.

As she spoke they saw David striding down the steps, dressed in a corporate suit and tie, his cell phone to his ear, a satchel over his shoulder, glasses perched on the edge of his nose. He waved when he saw them and then veered their way as he ended his call.

Mitch got out of the truck just as his cousin reached the vehicle. "Are you ditching work early today?" he asked as they shook hands.

David shook his head. "I left some paperwork at home this morning," he explained, and shook the satchel. "Hi, Tess."

She was out of the truck before Mitch had a chance to open the passenger side. "Hi, David. Is Annie around?"

"Inside with Scarlett."

Scarlett was David's daughter. Even though he was second cousin to David's kids, they called him uncle, and he suspected his own son would do the same.

"I'll talk to you soon," she said to Mitch, and walked toward the house.

Once she was out of sight, he turned toward his cousin. "When did life get so complicated?"

David laughed. "You're asking me that?"

Mitch sighed. If anyone would understand about loss and regret and trying to make a new life, it was the other man. Jayne, his late wife, had been a well-respected local aviator, and his mother, Sandra, had become like a second mom to Mitch and the rest of his siblings when their own mother died. She had been a pillar of support when Billie-Jack bailed. For a while, after losing Joss's wife, Lara, a couple of years earlier to cancer, combined with all the heartbreak he and Tess had endured, it had been as though the Culhane family were plagued by tragedy. But they'd rallied, pulling together, becoming a tight unit, relying on each other for support.

"I still care about her," he admitted with a heavy sigh.

His best friend nodded. "I know."

"How do I make the most out of half a life?"

David slapped him on the shoulder affectionately. "Smoke and mirrors, my friend."

Mitch laughed humorlessly. "It's that easy?"

"Not at all," his cousin replied. "But the alternative is to give up, right? If you care, hanging in is about all you can do."

Yeah, he thought as he headed back to the ranch. He just had to learn how to live with the fact that he still loved her.

And knowing she didn't love him in return.

Chapter Seven

Despite her reservations, and due mostly to Ellie's insistence, Tess finally agreed to a date for the baby shower.

On Friday they had talked for ages about the theme and the guest list, and she knew Ellie would have the entire event planned down to every detail. Tess still wasn't sure it was a sensible idea, but since it was over a month away, she put on a brave face and acted as though she looked forward to the event. The truth was, she was unsure how her return to Cedar River would be received. Mitch was well respected and well liked, and she was still the person who'd done the leaving and divorcing. She could certainly handle a little gossip, but didn't like the idea of dealing with confrontation about her reappearance in town. She couldn't live in a bubble either. She needed to get a job, form relationships, become a contributor to society for the sake of her son.

Her son…

Finding out the sex of the baby had cemented her belief that everything would be fine. That, combined with the support Mitch had displayed during the ultrasound, had given her a strong sense of peace about the baby. Everything would work out…she was sure of it.

She drove herself to the Triple C on Saturday for Clare's birthday party, declining David's offer to take her. She left the McCall ranch about twenty minutes after David and Annie, and when she arrived at the Triple C the party was well underway. The garden near the small orchard had been transformed into a fairy garden, with a white tent, lights and an assortment of activities to keep the twenty or so kids occupied for the afternoon.

She saw Mitch briefly when she arrived and he escorted her beneath the tent, finding her a seat beside her sister. Tess was glad that Annie was close at hand, but didn't want to burden her sister by having an emotional outburst. Not that she was likely to. Of course, she put all of her feelings down to baby hormones. She didn't want to think it had anything to do with her burgeoning feelings for her ex-husband. But she'd only been back a week and was more confused than ever. On one hand, he was being civil and supportive of her wishes, giving her time, without pressure, to think about the house Joss had offered. Plus, he'd taken her refusal to come back to him— *again*—with no resistance. Yes, he was perfectly polite and agreeable, and she should have been happy. But she wasn't…not really. Which made no sense. And which only amplified her confusion. She liked it much better when Mitch was being a disagreeable horse's ass and kept trying to get what he wanted. The easygoing version of her ex-husband, the one who didn't seem to have an agenda— kept her on edge. Which meant she hadn't rested properly for a couple of days, and was tired and irritable and wanted to sleep like a bear.

She also wanted to enjoy the party and was pleased with her inclusion in the day's activities. Despite her earlier thoughts about gossip and innuendo, no one seemed the least bit surprised by her return or the fact she was at a Culhane family function or the fact she was carrying Mitch's child. Destiny, one old acquaintance had called it. And Tess hadn't disagreed. Instead, she smiled and nodded and got drawn into a conversation about the ranch and local events, almost as though she'd never left.

There were two buffet tables, one laden with an assortment of treats for the kids, the other offering more substantial fare for the adults. And there were plenty of party games to keep everyone entertained.

Tess found a quiet spot on a bench seat by an apple tree and smiled when Shanook came up and sat at her feet. The orchard was one of her favorite places on the ranch and she enjoyed the moment. Plus, hanging out with Mitch's nieces was nice. And since her baby would be their cousin, Tess was eager to cultivate a relationship with the two girls.

"Having fun?"

She turned her head, halfway between spooning a second helping of cake into her mouth, and saw Mitch standing a few feet away.

Tess nodded. "Absolutely."

"I see you once again have my dog wrapped around your little finger," he remarked, and glanced toward the hound at her feet before he moved around the bench and sat beside her.

"He always liked me," she said as she touched the dog's head.

"Smart dog."

She saw his grin and it made her laugh. After spending time with him on Thursday, Tess realized she'd made a huge miscalculation. Hanging out with Mitch—laughing and talking and sharing moments about their baby that were so excruciatingly intimate— made one thing abundantly clear: she was not immune. In fact, she was as at risk as she ever was of being completely and utterly in love with him again, despite the resentment and the anger and the hurt she'd experienced when they broke up. Which meant she had a couple of choices—steer clear and make their relationship *only* about their child. Or rush back in. Both options terrified her. But there was something about the day—something that had everything to do with family and acceptance and being a part of the legacy that was the Culhanes' that kept her where she was. Despite their divorce, they were undeniably part of each other's lives again. Denying it was pointless.

"So, what have you decided about the house?" he asked.

Tess rested the plate on her belly. "I'm going to take it."

"Good, I'll tell Joss to arrange a lease agreement. And before you say anything, I fully intend paying for the house."

She tensed. "That's not necessary. I have savings, and I will return to work once the baby is—"

"Tess," he said quietly, "I will be supporting my son, and you haven't a chance in hell of changing my mind on this."

She knew some battles weren't winnable. "Sure, whatever you want."

He laughed softly. "That was an easy cease-fire. When would you like to move in?"

"The sooner the better," she replied. "I think I've imposed on my sister and your cousin for long enough. As soon as Joss says it's okay, I'll move, but I'll need to buy some new furniture and drapes and baby things."

"We can do that together."

Confusing idea. But she didn't say it. There was a niceness about the moment she didn't want to change. And, truthfully, she liked being alone with him, while listening to the delighted laughter of kids in the background and the animated chatter of the adults and the soft sound of music playing.

"How's the birthday cake?" he asked.

Tess passed him her plate and he finished it off in a couple of bites.

"Still like sweets, huh?" she asked.

He grinned. "I guess. So, have you told your mom and stepdad about the baby?"

"Yesterday. They are delighted about the idea of becoming grandparents. They're coming for Thanksgiving, and they'll also come and visit once he's born."

"How did your mom take the news about my…involvement?" he asked.

Tess sighed. "Mom always liked you. I think she's pleased the baby will be living in Cedar River."

He nodded. "Would you like to stay for a while after the party? We could do some online shopping for the baby."

It sounded cozy and domestic and very much like dangerous ground. Still, there were things she needed to share with him if they had any hope of having a reasonable and effective co-parenting arrangement. Plus, she figured if she met him halfway on some things, he might forget any idea he had about going for a formal shared-custody arrangement. And it wasn't as though he was bad company. In fact, there had been a time when he was all the company she had needed. Long ago, of course, but the memories lingered. And Tess was still susceptible to his broad shoulders and glittering green eyes and the deep sound of his voice.

"Sure, sounds like a good idea."

So, several hours later, after she'd mumbled something to her sister about staying behind to help clean up, ignoring the heat smacking her cheeks because she knew Annie could see right through her story, Tess found herself in the front living room with Mitch, sitting side by side on the sofa, surfing the net for baby things. Ellie had discreetly left them alone and returned to her cottage, and Tess suspected the younger woman thought she was playing cupid.

"We should just order two of everything," he said, and started making a list, clearly enjoying himself. "And I was thinking I need to buy a new car, since the truck isn't suitable for a car seat."

"You could get a minivan," she teased, and popped a couple of pieces of popcorn into her mouth. They were snacking on party leftovers, and Tess was more relaxed than she'd imagined she would be.

His brows rose and he looked sideways. "How many kids do you plan on having?"

The intimation could not be missed, and she colored hotly. "Just one."

His expression changed, and he grabbed her hand, speaking soberly. "Is your heart truly healed, Tess?"

She sucked in a sharp breath, knowing exactly what he meant. "Mostly," she admitted. "I mean, of course I think about what might have been, and I still grieve each baby I lost. But I think it will be easier once he's here with us and in my arms."

"I'm glad," he said softly. "I know how much this must mean to you."

"I know you do," she said, threading their fingers. "I might not have realized it at the time, but over the years I've had a lot of thinking time. A lot of reflection. I know I wasn't the only one grieving back then."

"It just felt like it?" he suggested.

She nodded a little. "Well, I know it's generally harder for men to talk about feelings and emotions and all the things that go hand in hand with loss and grief. I understand a little better now."

"The truth," he said, and raised their linked hands. "I felt utterly helpless. It wasn't something I was used to. Usually I can fix anything, but I couldn't fix you. I couldn't make it right."

"You don't have to, you know," she said, pushing a little further. "Make everything right, I mean."

"It's all I know."

"Occupational hazard," she said quietly. "Because everyone depends on you to be strong and always in charge and not to have any weakness."

"Something like that."

"So, you gave me an ultimatum instead?"

His fingers tightened. "I was desperate."

"That's quite an admission."

He shrugged, looking sheepish, but still gripped her hand. He looked at her mouth and Tess knew exactly what he was thinking. About kissing her. And about her kissing him. Which was exactly what she *was* thinking about but trying desperately not to show it. As nice as it would be, all kissing would do was confuse her more than ever. Because, despite their undeniable chemistry, they'd lost what they'd once had and only a fool would try to recapture it.

"Would you like to go out for dinner sometime?" he asked unexpectedly, and released her.

Tess stared at him. "Dinner? You mean, like a date?"

He nodded. "I thought we could spend some time together."

"We're spending time together now," she reminded him of the obvious.

"That's different," he said, and got to his feet. "This is about the baby. A date would be about…us."

There is no us…

The words teetered on the edge of her tongue, but she didn't say them. He was trying, and she had to give him credit for his restraint and his efforts. Still, knowing he had an agenda and wanted things his own way made her resistance linger. "I'll think about it," she said instead, and yawned a little. "I should probably go, it's getting late. I need to go home and take a shower and wash away the grime of the day. Hanging out with a bunch of nine-year-olds has proven to be exhausting."

It was dark outside, and she glanced at her watch and noticed it was past six o'clock. It had been a long day and she was tired. She was about to get to her feet when he held out a hand.

"Why don't you stay a little longer and rest? I'm sure we haven't covered all the things we need to buy for the baby's room. Make yourself comfortable and I'll make that chamomile tea you like. When you're ready to go I'll take you back to Annie's and get Wes to follow in your car."

It seemed like a terrible inconvenience, but she *was* feeling tired and her ankles were a little swollen, she noticed. "If you're sure it's not too much trouble?"

"No trouble," he said quickly. "Be back in a minute."

Once he left the room, Tess pulled her legs up onto the sofa and rested back a fraction. She looked around, noticing a lamp on in the corner where the Christmas tree always sat. She wondered if Mitch still decorated the house like he used to when they were married. It had been something they'd loved doing together. In fact, the whole family were part of the tradition. Christmas was a big deal for the Culhanes, and she figured this year would be no exception. Ellie and Joss in particular loved getting the house ready and they usually celebrated the event over several days. This year, she suspected, she would be a part of it, too, since her baby would be only a couple of weeks away from being born.

She sighed, stretching out her legs as she closed her eyes for a moment. Just a moment.

When Tess eventually opened her eyes, she was startled to discover she was laying on a bed. A very large bed. In an all-too-familiar room. Her old bedroom. She blinked a couple of times to adjust to the half light coming from the small lamp on the bedside table. The wide shutters that led out to the balcony were closed, and she noticed nothing was out of place in the entire room. And on one wall, by the sitting area, was her and Mitch's wedding portrait. She'd wondered where he'd had it moved to and hadn't considered the possibility of it being in their old bedroom. Which was the exact moment she realized he no longer slept in the room. Because nothing was different. Nothing had been touched. Even the duvet was the same as when she'd left it.

It was obvious she'd fallen asleep and he'd carried her upstairs. She had a vague memory of stirring in his arms as he'd moved her from the couch. She slowly swung her legs off the bed and sat up, taking a couple of breaths. She got to her feet, found her shoes and made a quick bathroom stop in the master bathroom. When she returned she noticed that there was a small pile of clothes on the end of the bed next to her tote. *Her* clothes, she realized, things she'd left behind four years ago. A pair of stretchy pull-on pants with a drawstring waist and a soft pink sweater. She glanced back at the huge bath in the master suite, mentally comparing it to the small shower cubicle at Annie's, and within a minute was back in the bathroom and filling up the tub. She spent a decadent half hour in the bathtub, using some of her old bath crystals that were lined up on a shelf and were still in surprisingly good shape. Once she dried off, she rummaged through her tote and found a spare pair of cotton underwear, dressed in the clothes that were left out, minus her bra, shoved her other garments back into her bag and headed from the room. There was a light on in one of the rooms down the hall and she made her way there, stalling in the doorway. The room had once been used for guests, but now she sensed it was Mitch's permanent bedroom.

"Everything okay?"

She turned and found him a few feet away, leaning against the wall, arms folded, his feet crossed at the ankles, dressed in jeans and a dark sweater that stretched over his shoulders like a second skin.

"I fell asleep," she said, feeling the intense intimacy of the space between them.

"You did. I carried you upstairs."

"And didn't break your back," she said with a small grin.

He chuckled. "I see you found the clothes."

Tess's skin warmed. "My old sweats. You kept them?"

He shrugged. "Habit."

"Why did you move out of the big room?"

His green eyes glittered brilliantly. "You know why."

Awareness and heat swirled between them like a chemical experiment out of control. It had always been that way, she thought. There was always a force bigger than them both pulling them together, making it impossible for one to truly ever forget the other.

"It will never go away, will it?" she said softly. "This thing between us."

"No," he replied, and pushed himself off the wall, moving closer. "Too much history. Too many feelings."

Tess swallowed hard, dropping the tote to her feet. "That afternoon in Sioux Falls… It was inevitable the moment we saw each other across the hotel foyer."

"Yes."

She sucked in a breath, saw his green eyes darken, felt her body go warm all over. "Like it's inevitable right now?"

He nodded and reached for her, curling a hand around her nape. "I think so."

Tess moved closer, feeling heat from him burn through her like a bonfire. When she was against him, when her belly touched him and her hands rested on his chest, he tilted her head and looked into her face. There was passion and desire in his expression, so intense it almost knocked her at the knees. And something else. Memory. Feeling. And more. Things she didn't have the courage to acknowledge.

But she knew what she wanted. What she needed. Even if it was just for a moment. Even if it would only complicate everything. Complicate them. Since that day in Sioux Falls, she'd missed Mitch's touch, his tenderness, the way only *he* had ever made her feel. And, of course, she'd missed him before then. Since the day she'd walked out on their marriage. And every day in between.

She pressed closer, stood on her toes and kissed his mouth.

It took only seconds for Mitch to kiss her back, and then his lips were moving over hers and his tongue was in her mouth and they were locked together in a heated embrace. Her hands moved to his shoulders and she gripped harder, pressing closer, finding comfort and strength within his arms.

"Make love to me," she whispered against his mouth. "I don't want to feel anything but you."

He stepped her backward until they were in his bedroom. He closed the door and tugged at her sweater, pushing off one shoulder, trailing kisses along her collarbone, finding the sensitive spot at her nape and lingering there, making her crazy with need. She'd heard stories about pregnancy amplifying libido, but hadn't experienced it until that moment. Tess moved her hands and found her way under his sweater, tracing her fingers across his stomach. He sucked in a sharp breath and moved, quickly pulling the sweater over his shoulders and tossing it aside. She absorbed the sight of him, every sinew and muscle, every inch of his taut skin. He kissed her again and again, going slow and then deep and anchoring her head passionately.

When her sweater disappeared, he groaned at the sight of her bare breasts, cupping them gently in his large hands, rolling each gently with his thumb. Tess gripped his shoulders and led him toward the bed. He sat down and positioned her to stand in front of him, her legs between his thighs, resting his hands at her hips. He kissed her breasts, caressing each in turn, taking one pert nipple into his mouth, and then the other, driving her wild as he inched down her pants and briefs in one smooth move.

"My God, you're so beautiful," he said, and palmed her belly gently.

Tess thrust her hands into his hair and urged him closer. "I don't want to wait," she whispered. "I want to feel you now."

He dispensed with his jeans with lightning speed and drew her down onto the bed. "Are you sure this is okay?" he muttered against her lips. "I don't want to hurt you."

"You won't hurt me," she assured him.

He nodded and kissed her, tracing his hand down her thigh, dipping between her legs and finding her ready for him. He caressed her intimately, drawing a response, creating an erotic rhythm that drove her wild. And he kissed her—hot, deep kisses that were so torturously intense she thought she might pass out. When the pleasure came, when it lifted her up and over into that place meant only for lovers, Tess cried his name, reveling as pulse after pulse of white-hot release surged through her veins.

When the vibrations abated, she reached for him, finding him hard and ready, and within moments they were joined together. He stayed above her, holding all his weight effortlessly on his strong arms, kissing her hungrily as they moved as one. When he shuddered above her, Tess held him, waiting for the release only he could give her, knowing she was still completely and undeniably in love with the only man who had ever had her heart.

Mitch waited until his arms were numb before he moved and rolled, hating how alone he felt the moment their bodies were apart. She was breathing hard, drawing in long gulps of air, and he took a few moments to draw enough air into his own lungs so he could speak.

"Are you okay?"

Her eyes were closed and she was smiling. "Perfectly fine."

He let his gaze linger at her breasts and then her rounded belly, and he fought the urge to lay his hands over their son in a primitively protective gesture. But everything about his feelings for Tess bordered on primitive. The bed coverlet was tangled at their feet, and he saw their clothes spotted from the doorway and across the floor. He figured only ten minutes had passed from the time he'd met her in the hallway and then smiled to himself when he realized he really needed a do-over to ensure he took his time and used at least some finesse, instead of being all eagerness and impatience.

"What?" she asked, clearly sensing his mood.

"That was something of a land speed record," he said ruefully. "I'll do better next time."

"I'm not complaining."

Her frankness turned him inside out. And turned him on. He grasped her chin and kissed her gently. "I didn't hurt you?"

She shook her head fractionally. "Of course not. But if you insist on doing better...be my guest."

He laughed and rolled her on her side, facing her, their baby between them. "Feel like having something to eat first? There's plenty of party leftovers in the refrigerator."

Ten minutes later they were downstairs eating cold fried chicken followed by copious amounts of cake and tea. The mood between them was oddly relaxed, surprising considering what had recently happened upstairs. There was none of the post-sex awkwardness they'd experienced in Sioux Falls. In fact, it felt very much like it used to when they were first married. Making love had always been part pleasure, part connection, part affirmation of their feelings for one another. Never a chore, never just about the physical act itself. Often, more emotional than physical, although he couldn't deny how damned good it felt to find release and solace in her touch. It had been nearly six months since they'd been together, and he hadn't been with anyone else.

Later, once the dishes were cleared, they headed back upstairs and made love again. He took his time, kissing and touching every part of her, anointing her skin with caresses that were whisper soft and designed to drive her crazy. She moaned and writhed and came apart in his arms, and Mitch thought how he'd never tire of hearing her moan in pleasure as release claimed her. There was something insanely erotic about watching the woman he loved reach orgasm and say his name as she climaxed.

Afterward, once his breathing returned to normal and he could feel his legs and arms, Mitch held her closely, splaying his hand over her belly and feeling their child move inside her. The intimacy was acute and heart wrenching, and it was hard to hold on to the swell of emotion surging through his system. She cried a little, too, he noticed, but didn't say anything. He simply held her and stroked her hair until she fell asleep in his arms.

When he awoke it was past six. Sundays were the one day a week he liked to sleep late—and six in the morning was late. Regardless of the day of the week, the ranch never slept and there was always plenty to do. But he knew Wes and the ranch hands would see to the feeding if he didn't make an appearance by six thirty and decided he'd much rather lie in bed with Tess than brave the cold morning air.

She stirred around seven thirty and her lids fluttered open. Her cell had been pinging intermittently most of the night and had already gone off twice since dawn. Her sister, he figured, and suspected she would have some explaining to do once she returned to the McCall ranch.

If she returned...

Things had changed quickly, no doubt about it. And with any luck, she'd see the good sense in forgetting any ideas about living anywhere else...or raising their son alone.

"Good morning," he said as she opened her eyes and blinked a couple of times.

She took in her surroundings, grabbing the sheet to cover herself. "Hi."

"Bit late for modesty," he said, and grinned.

She shrugged. "Did I dream last night happened?"

"Nope. I've got a hickey on my neck to prove it."

She looked mortified by his teasing. "Oh, God, I'm sorry. I didn't mean to—"

"I'm kidding, Tess," he said, grabbing her hand and kissing her palm. "Stop stressing. And we're grown-ups, we can do what we like. Want some breakfast?"

Color leached from her face and she sat up, dragging the sheet with her. "I should probably go before Mrs. B or Ellie realize I'm here and start asking questions."

Mitch's gut sank. "Mrs. B doesn't work Sundays and Ellie is probably already out riding her horse. Are we about to have one of those postmortem thingies?" he asked. "Because if we are, I need coffee and food first."

"Don't make fun of me."

"I'm not," he said, and kissed her firmly on the mouth. "I just don't want you getting all worked up because we made love. That's what people in a relationship do, Tess. And whatever this is…it sure feels like a relationship right this minute."

Her eyes widened for a moment and then she nodded. "Okay…no postmortems. For the moment. But I really should get going. Annie will be—"

"You might want to check your phone," he suggested. "It's been pinging since last night."

She groaned. "See…people are already talking."

"Does it matter?" he shot back and got up, pulling on his jeans. "People talk, Tess."

"I hate gossip."

"Then don't give them reason to. Come home."

Her mouth tightened. "I knew you'd be like this," she

said, and dragged the sheet with her as she got out of bed, draping it around herself toga style.

"Like what? Like I want you here, in my house, in my bed, where you belong?"

She rolled her eyes. "Stop being stupidly macho and turn around so I can get dressed."

He propped his hands on his hips. "You think there's some part of you I haven't seen, touched or tasted?"

Her jaw clenched and she dropped the sheet defiantly, quickly snatching up her clothes and getting into them in record speed. When she was done, she rummaged through her bag for a moment and then turned to face him. "Have you seen my car keys?"

"Downstairs on the coffee table in the living room," he replied. "Where you left them."

She was by the door, her fingers on the handle. "I know what you want, Mitch, and I know that it seem like the obvious next step."

"I want you here," he said, hands on hips, irritation churning in his chest. "Is that so impossible to comprehend?"

"You want your son," she corrected. "I simply come with the package."

"Don't be foolish," he said sharply. "Of course I want you. Didn't I prove that last night?"

"Sex is still just sex," she said quietly. "Even great sex. We fell out of love a long time ago and—"

"So, we try to fall back." He moved closer, aching inside at the knowledge she could dismiss their past so easily.

"And what if we don't?" she queried, her cheeks spotted with color. "What if this—" she waved an arm toward the rumpled bed "—what if this is all we ever are? I know you want our son to be raised here, and part of me wants that, too, but the other part," she said, and tapped her chest with her palm, "the other part knows you'll dish out some kind of ultimatum when things don't go your own way. And I don't want to live like that, always wondering if you'll say something, or I'll say something, or we'll disagree and say things to hurt each other. That's what we do…and I don't want to be that person, Mitch. And I don't think you do, either."

Anger and resentment curdled through his blood, because she was obtuse and unreasonable and didn't have the courage to at least meet him halfway. So, he went for it, trying to articulate exactly what was in his heart, without quite saying the words.

"I still care about you."

She gasped, stepping back, shaking her head. "No, you don't. You'll just say whatever you have to in order to get what you want. That's not love, Mitch. That's control. That's your insatiable need to make everything right in this perfect little world you've set up for yourself. Well, I'm not perfect. I never was. And that's what eats at you… knowing you couldn't turn me into the perfect picture of the wife you wanted, who would do and say all the right things. We were broken, and nothing could fix it. And years might go by and we can have a great time between the sheets, but the truth is, we're *still* broken. Now more than ever, because I'm not prepared to settle for less than a complete partnership. And you and I…we don't have that kind of dynamic. We never did."

She took a breath, long and hard and clearly filled with the same level of anguish he was feeling through to his soul. He watched as she left the room, dragging air into his lungs for a moment before he followed her down the stairs. He heard noise coming from the kitchen and checked his watch. Eight thirty. Joss had arrived with his kids, and the girls would be waiting for their weekly horse-riding lesson. Mitch enjoyed the time he spent with them, but today wasn't the day for family bonding. Today was the day he had to try to salvage what was left of his relationship with his ex-wife. He stood at the bottom of the stairs, saw her head for the living room and then heard his brother's voice.

"Tess's car still outside?"

He turned. Joss was ten feet away, grinning broadly. "Yes."

His brother laughed. "See, I told you. Back to basics always works. I won the bet, so you owe me a hundred bucks."

He was about to make some impatient retort when he realized Tess was now standing on the other side of him, her tote clutched tightly to her side. She was scowling, clearly interpreting the conversation.

"A bet?" she demanded.

He shook his head. "It's nothing. Forget it."

Her jaw clenched. She clearly didn't believe him and he couldn't blame her. It did sound bad. "You made a wager about us?"

"No," he said quickly, flashing his brother an impatient, go-away look.

"To see how long it would take you to get me into bed, I suppose." She clicked her fingers. "A week," she said, and laughed humorlessly. "You had better odds in Sioux Falls."

He scowled. "Can we talk about this privately?"

"You can talk all you want," she shot back. "I'm leaving."

"What you do best," he snapped, and then wanted to snatch back the words because he knew they were mean-spirited and hurtful. But, damn, he was hurting, too.

"See, there's that controlling arrogance in action. It's always your greatest motivator. And what *you* do best."

He made an impatient sound. "Tess, let's talk about this and try to—"

"I'll take your house," she said to Joss, cutting Mitch off and ignoring his plea. "But I'll pay my own rent and the moment you start taking money from him—" she hooked a thumb in Mitch's direction "—I'm out, understand?"

He saw his brother nod vaguely, as though Joss was as startled as he was by the strength and disdain in her voice.

Then she turned toward Mitch. "As shocking as this might be to you, Mitch, you don't get to call the shots in my life. You can have your fifty-fifty custody if that gives you enough control. Tell your fancy lawyer to draw up an agreement and I'll sign it. But you and I are done," she said, glaring at him. "And last night will never happen again. Why don't you lay a wager on that!"

Then she left.

Chapter Eight

Tess had to admit, the house on Mustang Street was exactly what she'd hoped for. Small enough that she wasn't roaming large rooms looking for company, and big enough that she wasn't tripping over her own feet. She'd picked a room for the nursery and Joss had offered to paint the walls for her. He was a good landlord, too. Not intrusive and yet willing to make any repairs or modifications she needed to be comfortable.

And his big brother stayed away. Just as she wanted.

True, Mitch texted her every couple of days to enquire after her health, but there was nothing remotely personal in his communication and it was always about the baby. Halloween came and went, and Tess was happy to be a part of the trick-or-treating festivities. Joss's daughters usually came by to see her each afternoon, and they sat and ate cookies she'd baked. Joss didn't say much when he collected the girls and Tess was grateful for his silence.

She didn't need any interfering Culhanes making her feel even more foolish than she did already. She was consumed with regret over her stupidity and rash behavior. She tried to rationalize it, and Annie told her to let herself off the hook and accept she'd made a mistake. Falling back into Mitch's bed had been a culmination of factors. First, their growing closeness during the previous week and how much the baby hormones were wreaking havoc throughout her system. Add in the fact she was back in a town where so much had happened to her on an emotional level, and of course there was the whole *Culhane* thing. Being at the ranch, hanging out with his family, being treated by his siblings and friends as though she had never left. It was easy to get swept up in nostalgia and familiarity and memories of what she had once had. Additionally, there was the whole online-shopping thing, forging closeness, creating intimacy, making her fall for him again little by little, hour by hour.

I'm an idiot...

So what if he'd carried her upstairs and acted all chivalrous and left out her clothes? She should have had more sense than to get swept up in some romantic notion based on lingering feelings and a love that had become lost. *And* she should have realized that Mitch was too smart to *not* have an agenda. And a wager, as it turned out. Joss had tried to apologize for his interference and she'd waved off his words, not wanting to get into anything with any of Mitch's siblings. The less they knew about her complicated relationship with him, the better.

On a bright note, she'd rekindled her old friendship with her neighbor, Lucy Monero, and Tess was pleased she had such lovely people around her. Annie, of course, texted daily and dropped by every couple of days, so she wasn't short on company. Except at night.

She'd been in the house for a couple of weeks and found the evenings the hardest to endure alone. It didn't make much sense, she knew, since she'd been alone for years in Sioux Falls, with a small circle of friends and work colleagues. Eventually, she figured she'd have that again, particularly after the baby came and she had the opportunity to join playgroups and other activities where she would meet people. Until then, she was content to hang out with her sister and keep a low profile.

She had settled into a rhythm, buying a little furniture, going for walks in the morning, arranging the nursery, tending to her garden in the afternoons. Making a life. *Post* Mitch. Even though they'd never really be done because they had a baby coming and their son would tie them together forever. She had to get some kind of routine going, even if it was merely a facsimile of a life. Pretending was okay. Pretending would get her through the hard days.

He drove her to her prenatal appointment in Rapid City and they talked about the baby, the weather, the new foals that were arriving soon—they talked about everything except their relationship. Her examination went fine and the baby was growing perfectly. He didn't touch her, didn't offer to wipe the gel from her belly, didn't do anything other than open the car door.

Three long weeks after her sleepover at the ranch, while she was pulling a few weeds from the flower bed at the front of the house one afternoon, an unfamiliar silver SUV pulled up outside her house. She stretched out her back and planted her hands on her hips just as Mitch got out of the vehicle and walked up to her gate.

"Nice rig," she said. "New?"

"And practical," he replied, and nodded. "How are you feeling?"

"Fine."

"Joss said he talked to you about the misunderstanding," he said.

"You mean the wager you had to see how quickly you could get me into bed?"

He tugged at his collar. "It wasn't like that, I assure you. Just Joss making some tactless, off-the-cuff comment. I wouldn't disrespect you in that way."

Emotion clogged her throat. Of course, she knew that. "You look terrible."

He ran a weary hand through his hair. "Lack of sleep can do that to a person."

"What's giving you sleepless nights?" she enquired, trying to look disinterested in his movements.

"You."

A surge of sympathy rushed through her blood and she relaxed her tight jaw. "I don't mean to."

"I know," he said. "Goes with the territory, I guess."

She wanted to ask *what* territory, but then wasn't sure she wanted to hear the answer. But she did want to know why he'd turned up. It broke the status quo. It put her on edge. For a moment she considered inviting him inside, but suspected he'd start insisting she needed more furniture and then want to go shopping. True, she did need more than the couch and coffee table and small sideboard that had arrived the day before, but she wasn't about to endure nesting advice from her ex-husband. And she didn't want him in her house, picking fault, looking at her in his lordly way, making it clear he wanted her back at the ranch, where he believed she belonged. "Is there something you wanted?"

"To make sure you were okay," he replied. "I sent two text messages this afternoon and you didn't respond. I was worried."

"My phone battery died. It's been charging all afternoon. But I'm fine, as you can see."

His gaze dropped downward. "Your belly has popped out this week."

"I know," she said, and touched her stomach. "I'm twenty-nine weeks now. And he's been kicking up a storm in here. I think he's a soccer player in the making."

There was a tense and awkward silence, and she noticed how he was fidgeting and his hands were tightly clenched. He looked as though he needed a haircut, too.

"I was wondering," he said quietly, his voice carrying a little on the late afternoon breeze, "if you'd like to go out tonight?"

Was he back to the wanting-to-date-her idea? Surely he knew that was impossible.

"I can't."

He stilled. "You mean, you won't?"

"Same thing," she replied. "With the same outcome. We don't need to date to be successful co-parents. And I told you we were over. I don't want to be on the *Mitch and Tess* merry-go-round anymore. Did you contact your lawyer?"

"Not yet," he replied. "But I will if that's what you want."

"I think it's probably best that we have a formal contract in place, don't you?"

"Is that what we've come to?" he asked rigidly.

"I'm thinking of the future." She crossed her arms, dropping her voice a little as an elderly man and his dog walked past the house and waved. "What if I get married again? What if you get married again and have more children? Do you think your new wife would be happy without a formal agreement in place?"

He gripped the gate. "I'm not getting married again.

And I won't be having children with anyone else," he said. "I told you that the day you left me."

The reminder of that awful afternoon cut deep. They had spoken so many hurtful words. Too many. And things, it seemed, hadn't changed. There was still anger and hurt between them, and she suspected there always would be. Sex and attraction didn't erase heartbreak and grief. All they'd done by making love was amplify the divide that had torn them apart.

"You can't possible predict that," she said, raising her chin defiantly.

"I can," he said, and touched his chest with one hand. "There's only so much room in here."

Tess's insides contracted. He looked unhappy. He looked exhausted. She knew he was as conflicted and confused as she was, but obviously for different reasons. He wanted what he wanted—control over his life and those around him. That was Mitch's way, and the way he'd been programmed to behave since he was young.

"I have to go," she said, and sighed as she turned to walk back to the house.

"Tess?"

She turned back and met his gaze. "What?"

"I never meant to hurt you back then," he said quietly. "I only wanted to protect you and our relationship."

"By threatening to have a vasectomy? How is that protecting me, Mitch? It was an ultimatum, your way of making me do what you wanted."

"I thought it would take away—"

"My hope," she said, aching inside. "My dreams. You shattered them, Mitch. You broke me into a thousand pieces and I can't forgive you."

"I loved you," he said. "I still do."

Tess's heart hurt. She couldn't bear hearing him say

the words. Couldn't bear thinking he still loved her—even though part of her longed for it like she longed for air in her lungs. Because they'd tried loving each other once, and it hadn't worked. It didn't matter that she loved him, too. He wouldn't change. He would always think it was okay to keep a part of himself locked up.

She took a long breath. "It doesn't matter anymore, because that's not really love, Mitch. Love is support and kindness and consideration. It's saying it's okay to be scared and feel lost and to be broken inside because the thing you want most in the world might never happen. Love is sharing that grief and opening up and being vulnerable. That's what I needed," she implored. "That's *all* I needed, Mitch…for you to be vulnerable. But you couldn't do that. You're incapable of vulnerability, because you think it's a weakness."

His gaze sharpened. She'd hit a nerve and they both knew it. Mitch didn't *do* weak. He was a mountain of strength. The glue in his family. Impenetrable. Unmovable. Rock-solid. A man of steel. And Tess needed someone who could bend with the tide. Someone who could embrace pain and grief and not be afraid to share that with her. That would never be Mitch. He would never falter, never yield, never be anything other than the stoic, unbending man who was in charge of everything, including his feelings.

"You wanted the impossible," he said flatly.

She shook her head. "No, I didn't. I wanted your raw truth. I wanted your hurt and angst and your pain. But you couldn't show me that part of you. Back then, all you could do was tell me how to feel because you didn't see *me*… All you saw was my grief. And you tried to control it by taking away the most important thing you could give me and I can't forgive you. I've tried," she admitted, and shuddered. "I've gone over it countless times, and I always end up feeling the same way—disappointed and hurt. And when you love someone, you should never disappoint them. And you should never steal their hope."

He stepped back, his green eyes glittering brilliantly. "I guess we *are* done."

She nodded. "We were done a long time ago. Sioux Falls was merely a blip."

"And three weeks ago?" he asked. "What was that?"

"It was goodbye," she said.

She waited for a moment, expecting him to say something. But he didn't. He turned on his heels and strode back to his vehicle. He disappeared from view quickly, and it took several moments for Tess to realize she had tears on her cheeks.

And to acknowledge that she'd never felt more alone in her life.

Late Friday afternoon the following week, Mitch took a call from Hank saying that a child had gone missing at the base of Kegg's Mountain and they needed help finding him. Shanook, clearly sensing something was wrong, was by Mitch's side the moment he grabbed his backpack and hiking boots, and within ten minutes they were on the road. He arrived at the camp in the recreational park at the bottom of the mountain around four o'clock, and Hank met him by the base that had been set up near several emergency services vehicles.

"Thanks for coming," his brother said, and shook his hand. "We estimate he's been missing for about five hours. He's seven years old, name's Emmett. He was fishing by the creek, his father fell asleep, curious kid wandered off… You get the picture. There were a few candy wrappers around the edge of creek, but we've no evidence to suggest he's gone into the water. I've had Willa Moon here with her hounds, but they haven't picked up any trace." Hank ran a hand through his hair, clearly frustrated. "I wish we had more daylight."

Mitch looked up at the late afternoon sky. It would be dark soon. And it was cold. And Kegg's Mountain was no place for a lost child. "We'll find him. Can I speak to his parents?"

His brother nodded and led the way to an ambulance where two clearly distraught people were hovering by the rear door. Hank introduced him, and Mitch asked a few questions about the child and then requested a piece of his clothing, specifically something he'd recently worn. The mother disappeared for a few minutes and while she was gone, the father, a man in his late twenties, quickly blamed himself for failing his son.

"What kind of a father am I? I can't protect my own kid. I should be out looking for my son right now instead of standing around talking. What if he's…" The younger man's words trailed off and Mitch spent the next minute reassuring him.

"If he's on the mountain, Shanook will find him," he said, motioning to the dog at his side. "The best thing you can do is comfort your wife. She's doesn't need to see you falling apart."

Maybe she does…

Maybe that was Mitch's number-one failing as a husband. He was so wrapped up in being a pillar of strength for his grieving wife, he'd forgotten how to *really* feel anguish and pain and bone-aching grief. Tess had done all the feeling. All the grieving. And he'd tried to rally his strength and be there for her instead of falling to pieces.

Too late now…

They were over. She couldn't have spelled it out any

clearer. He'd stolen her hope and her dreams, and she couldn't forgive him. He didn't need to hear that again in a hurry. They would be parents to their son, and that was all. She would get married to someone else. That's what she wanted. The love they'd once shared would be a dim memory.

And it hurt. It hurt so much he could barely breathe thinking about it.

He pushed away the thought when the man's young wife returned with a small red sweater. He took the garment, plus a two-way radio Hank passed him, saw that he had full service on his cell and shouldered into his backpack.

"I'll check in every half an hour," he assured his brother. "I'll do a sweep of the spot where he was last seen and go from there. Tell your men not to contaminate the area, will you?"

"Want me to come with you?" Hank offered. "Or perhaps you should take one of the EMT guys?"

"You're needed here," Mitch replied. "And you know I track better alone."

The young father stepped forward. "I can come with you. I need to do something."

Mitch held up a hand. "I understand your distress, but if your son is on the mountain, my dog and I will find him. The best thing you can do is to stay here in case Emmett wanders back by himself."

The boy's mother nodded, tears in her eyes. "He's only wearing a T-shirt and long pants," she said, and passed him a small olive-colored anorak. "Can you make him wear this when you find him?"

When, not if. He nodded and shoved the garment into the backpack. "Of course."

"And this," she said as pressed an inhaler into his palm. "He has asthma."

He nodded again. "I'll talk to you soon."

He called Shanook to heel, gave the parents a reassuring nod and headed toward the creek. He spotted a few emergency service personnel moving through the trees and undergrowth in formation and could hear Hank yelling out orders. The hounds from the other tracker were barking from the south, but once Mitch checked the edge of the creek and the footprint patterns, he was certain the child had headed toward the mountain. He knew the mountain well, had tracked it countless times as a boy and as a young man. It was one of the few things he'd learned from Billie-Jack. He'd found lost tourists before—this wouldn't be any different.

He pressed the child's sweater to Shanook's nose and the dog inhaled deeply, drawing in the scent as he was trained to do. Mitch unclipped his leash, ruffled his neck and motioned for the hound to go on ahead. The old dog headed directly for the east side of mountain and where several old mine shafts were boarded up. It was the one section of the mountain that was off-limits to tourists but would be catnip to a curious seven-year-old. Mitch trudged after the dog, scanning the undergrowth and finding a couple of twigs bent at odd angles. As he walked on, the hollers and sounds from the emergency service people grew fainter.

He tracked alone, without interruption, with only his thoughts and instincts and knowledge of the land and the earth. If Jake was around, he might have gone with him. His brother understood the land and the mountain like he did. Jake had had the same training from Billie-Jack, knew the same routine, had the same instincts, could read footprints and where the earth and dust had been disturbed.

He walked for half an hour, covering the ground

quickly, feeling the chill of the late afternoon seep through to his bones. It would be a cold night, too. Mitch came to an abrupt halt by a jut of sharp rock, noticing that Shanook was sniffing the air, searching for traces of the child's scent within the breeze. The hound groaned and dropped his head, running his nose along a few tufts of wild grasses. The animal stopped again, took a breath and looked back toward Mitch.

"Find something, old boy?" he said, and moved toward the dog.

Mitch examined the spot, then bent down to pick up a candy wrapper. The paper still held the scent of peppermint and had clearly been discarded recently. It was a good sign, what he needed to galvanize his instincts. Unfortunately, there were several old copper mines in the area, so he knew he'd need to check them out one by one. Once he was sure he was on the right track, Mitch decided he would call Hank and arrange for some of the emergency service people to help look for the boy. Until then, he didn't want untrained or clumsy feet walking over the child's tracks.

He checked in with his brother, registering Hank's insistence that he had people on standby to widen the search once he was sure the child was in the area, then headed farther up the mountain. The undergrowth was thick and unforgiving, and he stopped twice to pull splinters from Shanook's feet. The sounds of the other trackers had disappeared the farther up he went. Mitch was certain he was in the right area. Darkness fell and he pulled the flashlight from the backpack, walking slowly and avoiding tripping mostly from memory. He'd been in the same spot many times hiking with his brothers, and knew where he was from several landmark rock formations. Kegg's Mountain was steep and unforgiving and a good challenge for serious hikers. He covered ground for another thirty minutes, feeling the bite of the air across his face. Shanook came to a halt by a high mesh fence that had been erected to keep people away from one of the old mines.

He knew the mine and that it had ceased operating thirty years before. Mitch noticed a small gap in the fence where a tree had fallen and broken through the mesh, and then examined the ground around it, shining the light where Shanook was sniffing. Footprints. Small and erratic. And a candy wrapper. The dog howled and pressed his nose against the wire fence.

Mitch grabbed his cell and called Hank. "I'm at the old Pritchard mine, the one on the east face."

He heard his brother curse. They both knew how bad the mine was. "You find him yet?"

"No, but Shanook is howling, and you know what that means. Something or someone is here."

"I'll be there as soon as I can," Hank said. "Don't go near the mine shaft—that place has been unstable for years. I'll have help there in forty-five minutes."

"See you soon," he said, ignoring his brother's instruction.

Mitch grabbed the pocketknife from his backpack and cut through the wire, holding the flashlight steady under his arm. The wire snapped easily and he made a space large enough to fit through. The dog went through the gap first and he squeezed in behind, ripping his shirtsleeve on a jagged edge. He cursed, dabbed at the blood that seeped through the fabric and kept moving. He knew Hank would send emergency service people immediately, but Mitch wasn't about to leave a child in a potentially compromised position. The mines were treacherous for those who were unfamiliar with the terrain. What if it was *his* son in there? He'd be prepared to move heaven and earth to get him out, and he'd bulldoze over anyone who got in his way.

The entrance to the mine was boarded up and a large Danger sign was nailed to one side. He could see that people had been exploring the place, probably curious teens who were looking for a thrill. In the daylight there might be time to wait, but the night air was cold and, for an asthmatic child, very dangerous. He called the boy's name and waited. Nothing. Shanook made a low, growling sound, like he was on alert, cementing Mitch's suspicions that Emmett was close. He pulled at some of the boards, noticing a space wide enough for a small child to squeeze through. There were a couple of candy wrappers on the ground, pressed into the dirt, and he aimed the flashlight ahead, trying to make out shapes in the darkness. A bird called out overhead, making a long wailing sound and creating a haunting echo, and Shanook howled loudly.

"Steady, boy," he said as the hound came to heel at his side.

Mitch heard an odd sound, and then another, like dirt and stone shifting. It was clear the mine was unstable. He took a step forward, instructing the dog to remain where he was.

Support beams rumbled, as though the mine sensed his intrusion, and he felt dust flick down his collar. The sooner he found Emmett and got out, the better. His cell beeped and he checked the message immediately. It was Hank, informing him he had a team on their way to his location. The mine rumbled again.

"No time to wait," he said, and walked forward, scanning the darkness with the flashlight.

Mitch heard a sound, like a muffled cry. From behind him, Shanook barked. He knew the dog wanted to come forward, but he wasn't about to compromise the animal's safety. He instructed the dog to stay where he was, sterner this time, and the hound whined for a moment and then sat on his haunches, pawing the ground. Once he was satisfied the dog was settled, Mitch moved ahead, taking small steps, peering into the darkness, trying to distinguish between the shapes of old equipment and piles of rock debris.

The sound of heavy breathing came again, echoing around him, confirming what he suspected. "Emmett?"

He heard a squeaky croak, and then another, and he pushed forward, moving the light from side to side. The beam found something colorful—a T-shirt. Emmett. He made out the boy's outline and settled the light on his startled face for a moment, before dropping the beam to the side. The child was wedged between two rocks and was breathing heavily. His face was streaked with tears and dirt, but he looked okay, which was all that mattered.

The earth above moaned again and Mitch's chest twitched as debris shifted and dust fell into his hair. He had to get the child out, right now.

"Hey, buddy, your mom and dad have been looking for you," he said, and smiled.

"Are you a fireman?" the child asked croakily, wiping his face.

"No," he replied, stepping closer. "But my brother is a policeman and he asked me to help look for you."

"Is my daddy here?" the boy asked as Mitch approached.

"He'll be here soon," Mitch assured him, and was about to grab his cell when a loud shirring sound came from overhead and a shower of dirt and dust fell on his head and shoulders. It was as though the whole mine shaft was suddenly yelling for them to get out.

"We need to leave, Emmett," Mitch said quickly.

"I got stuck," he said, and pointed to his left foot, which was caught between two rocks.

From the entry, Mitch heard Shanook whining, clearly warning him to hurry. He shone the light down and saw that the boy's shoe was wedged between the rocks. Mitch took the child's arm gently and hauled him free. The shoe stayed, but he didn't waste time retrieving it, as the mine gave a loud and pitiful groan before more debris came showering down. His cell rang again, the sound reverberating in the small space, like another, sharper jolt, telling him to hurry.

Mitch gripped Emmett against his chest, crouching lower as they headed for the entrance, taking the deluge of dust and dirt onto his back and shoulders. Shanook barked, over and over, the yelps in unison with Mitch's steps. The entrance was ten feet away, but more rubble fell, heavier and harder, biting into the back of his neck. Mitch covered Emmett's face gently with a hand as dust flew into his nose and mouth.

Keep moving...

A loud sound turned his head and he glanced up for a moment. Several of the support struts were giving way, collapsing from the heavy weight of dirt channeling through any gaps and spaces it could find, working out a way to empty its belly into the void. A heavy beam came down, striking Mitch on the left shoulder and he dropped to one knee, releasing Emmett as another rush of dirt shot into his eyes. He braced the collapsing beam, pushing the child forward.

"Shanook...take!"

He pressed his back into the beam, feeling the heavy weight driving him down, watching as the terrified child lingered for a moment. Then Shanook ran forward, grasped the boy by the T-shirt and dragged him from the shaft. Once they were safe, relief pitched in Mitch's chest. Shanook wailed loudly, the sound pitiful as it combined with the sudden crush of rocks and dirt from above. Mitch felt a sharp pain in his back and his leg was forced into an excruciating angle. Something hit him from behind and he dropped to both knees, seeing stars, hearing white noise, feeling his chest and lungs tighten.

Tess...

The image came from some faraway place. He saw his wife, his child, his life rushing headfirst like a film reel on fast-forward as something else hard hit him in the middle of his back.

And then he saw nothing. Just blackness.

Chapter Nine

Tess was heading to bed on Friday night when her cell rang. It was an unfamiliar number, but she picked up and was startled to hear Hank's voice on the other end of the line.

"Tess…"

Her back straightened instantly. Police officers rarely called with good news. Her first thought was that something had happened to her sister and her entire body shook with fear. "What is it?"

"There's been an accident. Mitch is in…"

She couldn't recall much of the conversation. Something about a lost child and an old mine shaft and his brother being trapped and taken to the emergency room at the community hospital. After that, she was on autopilot for the next half an hour. Getting dressed. Grabbing her keys. Driving to the hospital.

When she reached the ER it was nearly nine o'clock. Joss, Hank and Ellie were in the waiting room. The twins were pacing, and Ellie was seated in the corner, her hands twisting in her lap. Her ex-sister-in-law was up and hugging her within seconds.

"It's so awful," Ellie said, tears in her eyes. "He's… he's…"

Dead.

"He's in with the doctors now," Hank said, and tapped her shoulder. "He was trapped under a pile of debris. It took an hour for the EMTs to get him out. We don't know much, but I think he broke his leg and some ribs and…"

Tess faded out a little and must have swayed, because within seconds Joss grabbed her arm and led her to a seat. She heard both brothers telling her about the accident, about how Mitch had saved a child's life, about how he took the full force of the collapse. As they spoke, her limbs and skin turned numb. It was a nightmare, it had to be. She was really at home in bed, dreaming, only *imagining* the worst. He was fine. He had to be fine.

Tess instinctively touched her belly, comforting her child. Mitch's son. She wanted to cry and scream and curse at the world. She wanted to make it all go away. She wanted a do-over of the last few weeks so they wouldn't end in the hospital. And Mitch wouldn't be fighting for his life.

Joss kept talking, Ellie cried, Hank began blaming himself and Tess sat by the door, waiting for the doctor to come and tell them he was going to be all right. David came into the room carrying take-out coffee. He nodded toward Tess and was muttering something about Annie giving her a call when Grant barged into the waiting room, in a suit and tie and looking like he'd come directly from his office.

"I got here as quick as I could," he said, and then jerked to a halt when he saw Tess. Of course, Mitch had told him about her return and about the baby, but she still registered the shock in his expression when he saw her. Long ago she'd been his schoolteacher, and then his guardian…and she cared deeply for him. Like she cared for them all. And she knew it was reciprocated. Grant didn't bother to hold back his emotions, and came toward her and hauled her into a tight bear hug. "I'm glad you're here," he said quietly.

Tess nodded. "Me, too."

Grant stepped back and looked at his brothers. "Tell me everything."

While they spoke, Tess returned to her seat, sent a quick text to Annie and tried not to overthink the situation. Tried not to imagine the worst. But it was hard.

It was another half hour before the doctor came into the waiting room.

Tess vaguely knew Kieran O'Sullivan. She knew he was a well-respected doctor and had recently married his high school girlfriend. She didn't know him well enough to read the expression on his face, but Hank, it seemed, did. Because he moved forward immediately and demanded answers.

"He's going into surgery now," the doctor explained. "There's an orthopedic surgeon driving from the hospital in Rapid City, and he'll take over and set the leg once the internal injuries are dealt with."

Tess's blood ran cold. "What kind of injuries?" she heard Hank ask.

He ran through a list and they all stood in silence, staring at the doctor, not believing what they were hearing. A badly broken leg. Internal bruising. Lacerations. Damaged spleen. A worrying head injury. Cracked ribs. It was too awful to contemplate. The doctor left them with the assurance that Mitch was in the best possible hands and he would return to update them soon.

"This is my fault," Hank said, once the doctor was gone. "I shouldn't have called him to—"

"He's the best tracker in the district," Grant said. "Who else would you call? No one knows that mountain like Mitch. I remember one time we were hiking past the plateau and he…"

Tess zoned out, the voices around her suddenly sounding like they were all stirring around together, making a kind of hazy white noise that was impossible to decipher. And she didn't want to hear, didn't want to listen to stories about Mitch as though they feared he wouldn't make it. He *had* to make it. They had a child coming. Their son needed his father. She wouldn't believe the worst, wouldn't imagine for one moment that he might not pull through.

And she didn't let the fear seep into her. Until someone said words that chilled her to the bone. Words that spoke volumes about the gravity of the situation. Words that no one in the room wanted to hear…because everyone knew what they meant.

And it was Joss who spoke them.

"Someone needs to call Jake."

There was a long, stony silence until Hank replied. "I'll do it."

Tess watched as Hank left the room and silence fell back upon them.

In the following hours, Tess had plenty of time to think, to go over every moment of her life in the last few weeks. Every argument. Every harsh word. Every hurt she and Mitch had inflicted on one another. And other things—every touch, every kiss, every moment she'd spent in his arms. And then, of course, the last time they'd spoken. Guilt settled between her shoulder blades. And regret. And an immediate wish for a do-over.

It was morning before they were told he'd come

through the surgery. Hank had arranged for a recliner to be brought into the waiting room so Tess could rest comfortably. But resting was out of the question. She planned on being awake when they took him into the ICU. What followed was a fraught few hours. He wasn't out of the woods, apparently. He'd come through the surgery, with his leg set and in a cast, plus repair done to some damaged soft tissue, and he'd lost his spleen. They were concerned about his head injury and were monitoring for any signs of swelling around the brain. He'd come out of the anesthetic but was heavily sedated. She heard words like *recuperate* and *shock* and *recovery*, and then something about the next twenty-four hours being important. They would administer medication to put him into an induced coma if they considered the head injury to be life-threatening.

When she was finally allowed to see him, she discovered he looked like he'd been hit by a freight train. He had a bandage on his head, a black eye, several cuts and nicks on his face and bruises everywhere. And he wouldn't be happy to know he'd chipped a couple of teeth.

His broken leg was propped up in a cast, and tubes connected his battered body to various IVs and monitors.

Joss and Hank had been in first, preparing her for what she was to see, but not even their grave expressions could make her ready. She swallowed back the acrid burning in her throat as she approached the bed. A nurse stood on the other side, fiddling with an IV line and writing something in his chart. The woman made eye contact and smiled gently, as though she knew Tess was barely hanging on. The room was darkened even though it was daylight outside, and the blinds were drawn.

Tess shuddered and touched his hand. His skin was cool, almost clammy, and she wondered if he was warm enough. He was asleep. Or unconscious. She wasn't sure.

Well, you said you wanted him to be weak and vulnerable...

He looked about as vulnerable as a person could get.

"If your husband wakes up," the nurse said quietly, "there are some ice chips in the cup on the side table."

Your husband...

Tess didn't register much else. Other than the "if" comment. What did that mean? That he might not wake up? That he was still critical? Surely he wouldn't be allowed visitors if he was in danger?

"Should he be awake now?" she asked, terrified of the answer.

The nurse shook her head. "No. I meant for later."

The nurse left and Tess sat down, finding a unmarked spot of skin on his arm and holding her hand there. She wondered, for a moment, if he could register her touch. And if he would want it. They'd parted badly the other day, with blame and recrimination, hurting each other.

Admit it...you did the hurting. He'd simply come over to ask you out on a date, and you shot him down like a duck in hunting season.

Her guilt amplified, but she didn't withdraw her fingertips, thinking, *hoping*, that the physical connection would help. Of course, the doctor had said to talk to him, too, but no words would come. She looked at his battered face, his bruises, and an acute sense of helplessness washed over her.

Over the years, she'd experienced fear. When she was a little girl and her father passed away, when she'd first gone off to college, when she moved to Cedar River for her first teaching position and didn't know anyone in the town... Even her wedding day had been fraught with nerves, as much as she'd wanted to marry Mitch. And, of course, those awful years when she'd been trying to keep one of their babies in her womb. But nothing in her life compared to the sickening and gut-wrenching fear she experienced as she sat beside Mitch's hospital bed. It seeped through to her bones, closed her aching throat, made her hurt in the deepest part of her soul.

"Any change?"

It was Grant standing behind her who spoke. She turned and shook her head. "Not yet. They're keeping him sedated for a while, to make sure his head injury doesn't cause complications. Remember he's not long out of surgery," she said, trying to give the younger man comfort.

Grant ran a weary hand through his hair. "What if he…"

Tess knew Grant couldn't say the words. And knew why. Out of all his siblings, Grant was the one who looked to Mitch as more of a father than brother. "He will," she assured him, and, feeling about fifty years old and comforting a grown-up child. Her child. And, really, even though she was only thirty-one, Tess mostly felt like an entire generation removed from Mitch's siblings. Necessary, she suspected, from when she and Mitch were living together at the Triple C.

"The family needs him," Grant said softly. "He's the glue that keeps up all together."

She knew that. Without Mitch, the Culhanes would have been fostered in social services when Billie-Jack left.

"He'll come through this," she assured him. "Your brother is the strongest man I know. He's not going to let this beat him."

Grant nodded and told her that Joss had gone home for an hour to collect his daughters from his in-law's, and

Hank was at the police station and would return soon. Ellie was asleep in the waiting area with David.

"Why don't you go home and get some rest?" he suggested. "I'll stay."

Tess shook her head. "No, I need to be here, you know," she said, and touched her belly, "for when he wakes up."

"I understand," he said softly. "I know he'd want you here."

Tess wasn't so sure, but she didn't say it. She didn't want anyone to tell her she was right, that she had no place at Mitch's bedside, that he wouldn't want her support or prayers. That he'd tell her to go, to stop pretending she cared, that she was only at the hospital out of guilt.

But I do care...

She cared so much. And the notion he would never know it, that the last words they had said to one another were fraught with anger and bitterness, made her hurt so much she could barely breathe.

Grant left shortly after, saying he needed coffee and was going to the cafeteria to stretch his legs. Tess rested in the chair by Mitch's bed, her hand still on his arm, finding comfort in touching his skin and hearing the rhythmic sound of his breathing. She closed her eyes, and her other hand rested on her belly.

As her lids grew heavy, she relaxed a little, finding solace in the sounds and the dim lighting. From outside, she could hear other sounds, people talking in low voices, echoing footsteps that became a soothing melody, and she sighed, her heart rate slowing down. She thought she heard the door open. A nurse, she mused, keeping her eyes closed. Someone was in the room. She heard a deep voice. Not Mitch's, someone else. She knew it, but didn't have the energy to make it out. Then the voice was gone and all she heard was Mitch's steady breathing. When he woke up, things would be different. They would talk, sort things out, make it work. They had to for their son. Nothing else mattered except Mitch recovering and being a father to their child.

"Please wake up," she whispered, keeping her eyes closed. "I can't do this without you. Our baby needs you. I need you. Please come back to me."

He stirred and she was certain she heard a faint moan. And she hoped, gripping his arm, that her pleas would be enough. Because she couldn't imagine a world without Mitch in it. *Her world.* The last fourteen hours had been some of the worst of her life. Her baby needed him. She needed him. Tess just hoped, with all her heart, that she'd get the chance to tell him so.

Mitch couldn't believe how much it hurt to simply breathe. Flashes of memory banged around in his head. The mine shaft. Emmett. Shanook. Dust. Rock. Blackness. *Tess...*

He moved his fingers. Thank God they worked. And his toes. Some movement, but his left leg felt like a deadweight. He swallowed and felt razor blades in his throat. And his right cheek and eye socket felt like he'd gone ten rounds in the boxing ring.

"Mitch?"

Tess's soft voice cut through his thoughts and he took a breath, opening his left eye, very aware that the other was clamped shut and bandaged. "Hey."

"Thank God," she whispered, and let out a shuddering breath. Then the scent of her perfume assailed his senses and he felt her fingers against his arm, digging in gently. "Would you like some water?"

He tried to nod and failed, and within seconds a few soothing ice chips were placed against his mouth. He took them, letting the ice melt, and then swallowed. "What's the damage?" he rasped out.

She came closer, bending over him, and he could see her in the dim light. She looked pale and so tired. "Broken leg," she began, and then rattled off his list of injuries. "And they took your spleen."

"Is the boy okay?" he asked, wincing as pain shot through his limbs.

"He's fine," she assured him. "You saved his life. His parents have been asking about you. They're very grateful."

"Shanook?"

"He's home safe. He hurt his paw, but nothing serious."

Mitch relaxed, glad the child was safe. "I guess my dancing days are over for a while."

"A little while," she said, and touched his forehead. He wanted to flinch. He wanted to ignore the comfort in her touch. "I should go and tell your brothers you're awake. And David and Ellie…they'll want to see you."

"And Jake," he said, and closed his good eye. "Jake was here."

She shook her head. "I think he's still on his way. Hank called him and—"

"He was here," Mitch insisted. "I know he was here."

She put more ice chips against his lips. "Get some rest and I'll be back."

He closed his eye and tried to nod, too weary to disagree. Moments later a doctor and nurse came into the room. He listened as they talked around him, hearing Hank's voice, and Ellie's and David's. The people he cared about. His family. For a moment, he wondered if he'd dreamed Tess being in his room when he woke up, or her soft touch and her quiet voice.

But no, not a dream, because her perfume lingered

in the air, stronger to his senses than the antiseptic and usual hospital scents. The steady beep of monitors was oddly soothing among the talking and discussion. The doctor asked him a few questions and he answered the best he could, mostly with nods and unsteady grunts. The nurse checked his pulse, the doctor scribbled something on his chart, and he heard his family murmuring words to one another.

An hour later, after family came and went, after the nurse returned to do his vitals again, and the surgeon dropped by to relay the great news about his leg needing to be in a cast for at least six weeks, Mitch felt as though his head was going to explode. He'd been conscious for less than ninety minutes and had already had enough of hospitals and medical staff and well-meaning relatives sighing and smiling and making noises about how relieved they were he was going to make it. Like there had been doubt.

Our baby needs you. I need you. Please come back to me.

Tess's words came rushing at him. Words he'd heard from some faraway place. Words that had made him stronger, determined, ready to return to breathing and living. Ready to leave the pitch-black void he'd been in the moment the mine collapsed.

And then he knew, of course, that she didn't mean them. How could she? She'd said they were done. They had the baby to keep them connected and that was it. She couldn't forgive him. He'd stolen her hope. Broken her dreams. He needed to get a lawyer. Yeah…she didn't mean any of it.

As the nurse left, the door opened and Mitch opened his eye and saw his brother Jake walk into the room. Still sporting his military crew cut, he looked as familiar as always, and Mitch was very happy to see him. Jake would understand.

"You look like hell," Jake said, and stood by the end of the bed. "Rough day, hey?"

"You could say that," he replied hoarsely, and smiled and then winced because he hurt all over.

"Someone told me you saved a kid's life," Jake quipped as he sat down.

"Shanook did most of the work," he said.

"That old dog still hanging around you," he laughed. "Thought he'd have more sense than that. And you," his brother said, and frowned. "I heard that Hank told you not to go into the mine shaft?"

Mitch tried to shrug, failed and sighed. "Since when do I ever do what anyone tells me?"

"Never," Jake said. "You could have been killed."

"That's rich coming from someone who did two tours in a war zone."

"That was different, I was kind of fighting for my country."

"And I was trying to save a child. Anyway, you came all this way for nothing. I'm fine and the doctor said I'll make a full recovery."

"A long recovery," Jake corrected. "You'll be here for a week, at least."

"Don't remind me," he groaned. "The ranch won't run itself. There are two more Alvarez foals due in the next week or so and I—"

"Wes will keep things under control. And I'll be hanging around until you are out of here and back home. And Ellie will be on top of any issues that come up. Time for you to stop thinking about anything other than getting back on your feet."

Mitch made an impatient sound. "I'm gonna hate this."

Jake nodded. "Yep. And you're going to be a pain in the ass about it."

He didn't deny it. "It's good to see you. Almost worth getting crushed by that mine."

Jake smiled humorlessly. "I thought it was time I came back."

"Back? But not *home*?"

His brother shrugged. "It's just temporary."

Mitch sighed, fatigue settling over his bones. "It's still good to see you, temporary or not. I should probably rest for a while."

Jake got to his feet. "I guess you want Tess to come back in."

He closed his eye. "Whatever."

"She's outside."

He didn't want to see her, didn't want to see the sympathy in her eyes and the fake concern. "Later. I need to sleep."

"By all accounts she didn't leave your side when you came out of surgery."

He wanted to shrug like he didn't care. "It's not real."

"Looks real enough," Jake remarked.

"We're over," he muttered.

"You sure?"

He couldn't nod. "Positive."

"You've got a baby coming."

"Not enough," he said, the words hurting. "She made that clear."

His brother left the room, and since he was without an audience, Mitch was able to grunt in pain for the first time since he'd woken up. Everything hurt. His bones, his skin, even his hair. And he was damned thirsty. He couldn't move his busted leg and his head felt like a deadweight on his neck.

He had about ten minutes alone before Tess entered the room. She didn't say anything, didn't make a sound. But her perfume was unmistakable. She sat in the chair and Mitch pretended to be dozing. He didn't know what to feel, what to think. He knew he didn't want to talk about the accident, his injuries or anything else. Particularly about how she'd said she needed him, how she'd begged him to come back to her with such a yearning in her voice that he had experienced a pull toward her so intense, so incredibly strong, that instinct made him try harder, push more, to return from the dark place that threatened to consume him when the rocks and debris had knocked him out.

He only wanted to sleep. He took a long breath, ignoring the way her hand came to lay against his arm. And, surprisingly, he did sleep.

When he awoke, Tess was still beside his bed, still holding his arm.

"Hey," she said, and gave him some ice chips. "You've been asleep for a while. How do you feel?"

"Like I had a head-on collision with a bus," he croaked out.

She smiled and stood. "I'll get the doctor to—"

"No doctors," he insisted, and swallowed the melted ice chips. "I'm hungry."

Her smiled widened. "What would you like?"

"Cheeseburger."

"I was thinking soup and Jell-O."

Mitch felt like an invalid. And he hated Jell-O. "No Jell-O."

He was about to relax again when the door opened and Ellie, Hank and Jake came into the room. A minute later, Joss arrived with his girls, and David, his two kids and his stepfather, Ivan, also entered. He was pretty sure there were way too to many people in the room. It was a little claustrophobic, but he tried to smile and pretend he was happy and not as broken inside as he was on the outside.

"We were given permission," Ellie said, clearly reading his expression. "To come in here en masse. Tess did try and talk us out of it," she added, and looked at Tess briefly. "But we wanted to see for ourselves how much better you were."

He glanced toward Tess, unable to move his neck but catching her gaze with his open eye. Her mouth was set in a tight line, her hand on her stomach. Something flashed between them, a kind of heightened awareness of the situation, of the ridiculous number of people who were crammed into the small room, of the obvious tension between him and his ex-wife that no one seemed to notice except the two of them. It was always that way. They'd forged that connection years ago on the very first day they'd met.

The nurse arrived and quickly ushered everyone out… except Tess.

It seemed odd, somehow, that she was given the free pass to stay. Surely the nurse knew they were divorced, that they were busted, broken, not a couple. Sure, they had a child coming that would bind them together forever, but Tess wanted to marry someone else. She'd said so.

The nurses and doctors shouldn't assume he wanted her standing a vigil by his bedside simply because she believed he was going to die. Or his family. Hell, they'd probably put her up to it. He could certainly imagine his brothers asking her to say whatever she needed to say to get him through surgery and recovery. To get him back.

I can't do this without you. Our baby needs you. I need you. Please come back to me.

"The doctor will be back soon," the nurse said, and

checked his chart again. "He'll answer any questions you both have."

Both...

There was that *couple* thing again. They weren't a couple. He wanted to shout out the words, but his throat was filled with razor blades. The doctor arrived and ran through his list of injuries again, including the fact he'd he unable to bear weight on his broken leg for a minimum of six weeks.

"That's impossible," he said, and groaned. "I have a ranch that doesn't run itself. If I can't get around and—"

"Mitch," Tess said quietly. "You have to do what's best for you."

What's best for me is for my ex-wife and the woman who is carrying my child to stop pretending she gives a damn...

He grunted, ignoring her and forcing his concentration to stay with the doctor, who was rattling on about something called aquatic therapy once the cast was removed, about staying sedentary while his ribs healed, about stitches that would need to come out, about checking his vision wasn't permanently impaired in his right eye. Then about being transferred from post-op to the regular ward and being in the hospital for the next week, followed by complete bed rest for a couple of weeks after that. Tess asked a few questions and Mitch switched off, staring at the ceiling, wondering why everyone suddenly seemed to think it was okay that his ex-wife was discussing him as though she had some kind of claim on him...on *them*.

Once the doctor left, Mitch opened his eye and spoke. "Why are you here?"

She was by the bed, staring down at him. "To help."

"I don't need help."

She waved a hand in an arc. "Yes, you do."

"Then I'll get my family to help."

She was silent. "I was only trying to—"

"I get it," he said wearily. "You want to help. You can help by leaving."

"You don't mean that."

"I do."

She sighed. "I'll come back later."

"Don't bother."

She gasped. He heard it, but didn't see it. His good eye was closed. Like he also tried to close off his ears, his brain, his heart. He didn't want to hear her breathing or smell her perfume.

"Mitch… I…"

"We're done, remember? Broken. Over." He took a breath, one that hurt so much he had to use all that was left of his strength to *not* cry out loud. "Go home, Tess. Leave, remember how it's what you're good at."

He heard her sigh heavily, heard her walk across the room, heard the door open and then close. The moment she left the room he was consumed by a sense of emptiness that rocked him bone deep. Because the last thing he wanted was for Tess to leave his side. And, more than anything, Mitch wished he had the courage to ask her to stay.

Chapter Ten

Of course, Tess didn't leave him alone. She couldn't, despite his insistence she go away. She stopped by the hospital every day until he was discharged. If he refused to see her, she would sit in the family waiting room, chatting with whoever happened to come and see him. The only time he cracked a smile with her was when she arranged for Emmett and his parents to come and visit before they headed back home from their vacation. He was clearly puzzled by her insistence on hanging around, but she didn't care. All that mattered was Mitch getting out of the hospital and then getting back on his feet.

Eight days after the accident, he was released. Tess arranged for an ambulance to drive him back to the ranch, followed by Hank's patrol car and Joss's tow truck and Jake's hog. It was quite a motorcade and she knew it irritated him no end. Mitch didn't like fuss and didn't like being the center of attention.

And he certainly didn't like seeing her standing on

his porch when he was escorted via wheelchair up the temporary ramp that Jake and Ellie had had installed a few days earlier.

Shanook greeted him the moment he arrived and Tess noticed he actually cracked a smile when he was reunited with the old dog. His brothers and sister fussed around him and she couldn't help smiling a little when he said there was no way he was being *carried* upstairs.

"Don't be a horse's ass," Joss said, and grinned. "You can't sleep on the couch downstairs. You'll be more comfortable in a real bed. Doctor's orders."

"There's a roll-out bed in my office," he said flatly. "I can sleep on that."

"Nope," Ellie said, hands on hips. "You're liable to break your other leg trying to maneuver yourself in the bathroom with a wheelchair. Don't be a pain in the neck. The bathroom upstairs is big enough for the wheelchair. You know I'm right."

It took about five more minutes of reasoning to get him to agree, and Tess stayed out of the way while Joss and Hank lifted him from the chair, his broken leg suspended by Jake. She remained in the kitchen with Mrs. Bailey and helped prepare lunch for everyone. When his brothers came back downstairs they were smiling, except for Jake, who looked grim.

"He's unbearable," Joss laughed. "I feel for you, Mrs. B, having to put up with him for the next few weeks. When's the nurse arriving?"

"They're not," Tess said quietly, and covered the tray she'd prepared with a cloth. "I'm moving back in to take care of things until he's able to get around. You know he'll never agree to a nurse," she said, with a raised brow.

"I'm not sure he'll agree to you, either," Jake said flatly. Tess ignored the annoyance spiking through her blood.

Jake was clearly only saying what he believed Mitch wanted. And Jake, who was always Mitch's closest ally, would never fail to have his brother's back.

She grabbed the tray and looked at him. "I have to do this."

"The last thing my brother needs is more stress."

She nodded. "I know. I also know he's not happy with me right now. The truth is, we're not happy with each other. But we have a baby coming, and I'm not about to let my child's father recuperate from an accident that could have killed him, without doing *something* to help him through this. Even if he wants me to leave him alone."

She took a breath and rounded out her shoulders, seeing their startled expressions. Of course, they knew she wouldn't be talked into leaving. The Culhane siblings might close ranks around their brother, but they knew she wouldn't be swayed when she wanted something. And the reality was that, divorce or not, for a while she had been a Culhane. And that meant something to the people in the room.

For the next couple of weeks, it would mean everything.

She left the room and headed upstairs, stalling when she saw that he'd been put in the master bedroom. She lingered in the doorway, watching him as he sat up in the bed, his cast propped up on pillows, wearing a T-shirt and sweats with one leg cut out to make room for the cast. He was flicking stations on the television impatiently. Tess took a deep breath and entered the room.

"I brought lunch," she said cheerfully, and laid the tray at the foot of the large bed.

"I'm not hungry," he said irritably.

"Are you sure? It's been a long time since that hospital breakfast," she said as she looked at him. His eye was much better, not as swollen and now a delightful mix of shades of purple and blue and yellow. And the scrape down his cheekbone was healing nicely. The doctors were confident there was no chance of his head injury causing any ongoing problems, either. All he needed to do was rest and let his body mend itself.

"Are you comfortable?" she asked quietly.

"No," he replied. "And if I must be upstairs, I'd rather be in my own room."

"This is your room."

"This was *our* room," he reminded her. "And I'd prefer not to have to look at that twenty-four hours a day," he said, motioning to their wedding portrait hanging on the wall.

"I could ask one of your brothers to take it down," she suggested.

"Great idea."

Tess stared at him, stung by the bitterness in his tone. "Are you saying that to punish me?"

"Maybe," he said. "That's what we do, isn't it? You've been saying it all along. All we seem to do is be cruel to one another, over and over again."

Pain seared through her. Because his words hit home.

"Can't we have a do-over, Mitch?"

"To what end?" he asked, trying to sit up against the pillows and wincing in pain. "So you can make peace with yourself? I get it, Tess. I could have died in the mine shaft, and the last conversation we had was one about how we are nothing to each other. A blip, remember?"

Tess twisted the cap of the water bottle on the tray and moved around the bed, placing it on the bedside table. "I'll come back later, when you're in a better mood."

She managed a tight smile and left the room, heading down the hallway and walking into the room they had talked about turning into a nursery. She opened the overnight bag on the edge of the bed, extracted some of the clothes and hung them in the wardrobe. She'd packed the bag that morning, enough clothes and personal items for a few days. If she lasted that long. Mitch was about as welcoming as an arctic winter. He didn't want her at the ranch. Or in his life. The truth was, he could barely look at her. She laid out her pj's on the bed, placed her toiletries in the adjoining bathroom and then went back downstairs.

Jake was in the kitchen, sitting alone at the big table, drinking coffee.

"Where is everyone?" she asked, and flicked on the kettle to make tea.

"Mrs. B headed back to her cottage, Ellie and the boys are in the stables looking at the new foal."

"Chica had her baby, the latest Alvarez foal?"

He shrugged, looking surprised she knew the details. "I guess. Ellie insists on taking pictures to show Mitch. They'll be back soon."

"I get the feeling you want to say something to me," she remarked, popping a tea bag into a mug.

She met Jake's penetrating gaze. "He's pretty messed up."

"Well, a week ago he was almost killed, so yes, he is."

Jake shook his head a little. "That's not what I meant. I meant in here," he added, and tapped his temple. "I know my brother. I know when something is on his mind. Usually it's just the ranch and this family. But at the moment, it's something else."

Tess patted her stomach. "We have a baby coming, so naturally he's a little preoccupied."

"I know he wanted you back," Jake said bluntly. "And that you told him to get a lawyer."

Wanted. Past tense. "I want what's best for my child," she said.

"And do you think keeping Mitch away from his son is what's best?"

"That's not what I intend on doing," she replied defensively. "He can see as much of the baby as he wants. I've agreed to fifty-fifty custody."

Jake's expression softened. "Look, I know it's none of my business, but I'm concerned about my brother. And maybe having you here isn't going to help him recover."

So there it was...what he really wanted to say. And probably what everyone else was thinking.

"Is that how you all feel?"

He shrugged. "I don't think Mitch has said much to the others. And you know Ellie and Grant adore you, Tess. The truth is, none of us understood why you left in the first place. Mitch simply said it was his fault, and we accepted what he said. And then out of the blue, you're back and pregnant. I think we have the right to be a little concerned, don't you?"

She wanted to be annoyed, but couldn't be. The Culhanes were a tight unit. She had known that going in and accepting Mitch's proposal so long ago.

"I understand," she said tightly. "And I would never deliberately hurt your brother."

It was a lie. Because they did hurt one another. Maybe not deliberately. But sometimes she felt as though she said things to wound and punish him for not being *present* in their grief all those years ago.

Hank and Joss returned to the house and headed upstairs to check on their brother before they left. Ellie hung around in the kitchen with Tess, helping to clean up after lunch.

"Everything okay, sister-in-law?" she teased as she stacked the dishwasher.

Tess managed a playful scowl. "You probably shouldn't call me that anymore."

"I can't help it," Ellie admitted. "I'm still that little kid who wants her parents to stay together." She sighed. "I know you're not my mom. But...you were the only mom I remember."

Tess squeezed Ellie's shoulder. There were only seven years between them in age, but most days it felt like an entire generation. And she knew how much the younger woman looked at Mitch as a father figure. "We'll see," she said, and waved a hand.

"Does that mean you're thinking about moving back in permanently?"

She shrugged. "Mitch and I need to work things out between us, and figure out a way to co-parent our son," she said, and smiled warmly. "And you."

Ellie laughed. "I can be a brat. But I mean well. I meant to talk to you about the baby shower. I'll need a final list of who you would like me to invite. Annie said there would probably be a few old college friends you might want to come."

Tess half listened as Ellie prattled on about the baby shower and agreed she'd make a note of anyone she wanted on the guest list. Once they finished cleaning up, Ellie headed back to the stables and Tess returned to Mitch's room. The tray of food was untouched and she noticed how the wedding portrait was conspicuously absent from the wall and figured his brothers must have taken it down.

"You really should eat something," she said from the doorway.

He was watching the television and muted the volume when he spotted her. "I'll eat later."

"Ellie showed me pictures of Chica's baby. She looks adorable. What will you name her?"

"No point," he replied. "It's a filly, and the first filly goes to Alvarez. She'll be transported once she's weaned."

Tess entered the room and walked toward the French doors, pulling back the curtains. "Would you like the doors opened for a while?"

"Do you want to add pneumonia to the list?"

She raised her brows. "Really? Is every conversation going to be an argument?"

"You tell me," he replied. "You're the one intent on playing nurse."

"You need someone to look after you while you recuperate," she reminded him. "Would you rather we hire someone?"

"Yes," he quipped, then shook his head. "No. Frankly, I just want to be left alone."

"That's your frustration talking," she said cheerfully. "Would you like your laptop? A book? Magazine?"

"No, and stop fussing."

"Someone needs to."

"Not you."

Tess planted her hands on her hips. "Why are you being such a stubborn jerk about this? You don't want any help—you made that very clear. Give everyone a break, Mitch," she said. "We just want to help."

"By treating me like an invalid?"

"Could you at least try to stop being so damn negative about this and relax? Everything here is under control. Ellie and Wes can run the ranch, and Jake's here to help out for the next week or so. For once in your life, Mitch, let someone look after you for a change."

"Someone?"

"Me, okay?" she said, exasperated.

"I'm not good at being—"

"Vulnerable?" she finished for him. "Yes, I know. But sometimes it's okay to let someone else be in charge. It's okay to fall apart."

"I wouldn't know."

She knew that about him. "Well, I'm here if you want to talk."

He laughed humorlessly and she knew it hurt his healing ribs. "Since when did we ever talk?"

Tess ignored the hurt in her bones. He was in pain, feeling isolated and obviously wanted someone to vent at, and she was the closest target. She spotted his cell phone on the dresser and placed it on the bedside table, plugging it in to charge. "Try to get some rest."

She was by the door when he spoke her name.

"What?" she asked, and turned.

He exhaled heavily. "I don't want to sound ungrateful, but I'd prefer you to be honest about why you're here."

"You know why," she said, her hand against her chest.

"Guilt," he said without emotion. "Duty."

He was right. But there was another reason, growing ever more inside her. She was just terrified to speak the words out loud.

Because I love you...

And she did. But she was afraid of that love, too, terrified they would end up back where started.

Or worse...where they ended.

Mitch tried watching television, doing admin work on the laptop, even playing solitaire. But he was bored out of his mind, and it was only day one of his forced incarceration. He hated self-pity and he hated weakness, two things he seemed to be feeling abundantly at the moment. And he hated that everyone seemed to think they knew what he needed. What he needed, and wanted, was to be left alone.

Which would be great, if he could get to the bathroom by himself. Thankfully, Jake stopped in and helped him into the wheelchair every few hours. It wasn't easy, but he'd be damned if he'd admit he needed help. Mrs. Bailey dropped by after four to collect his tray, most of which was untouched. She tutted at his lack of appetite and said she'd return later with dinner. He managed a smile, and spent the next hour listening to the sounds of the ranch, which magnified his sense of helplessness. Sure, he was grateful to be alive, but the thought of being bedridden and out of action for weeks was unbearable.

And the idea of Tess sleeping down the hall was also out of the question.

She had to leave. Which was exactly what he planned on telling her when she showed up in the bedroom at eight o'clock, except he took one look at her and he couldn't speak. She wore a soft blue dress with tiny white flower sprigs on it that was cut out over her shoulders and came to her knees, stretching over her rounded belly. Her feet were bare, her blond hair was loose, her face devoid of makeup, and he thought he'd never seen her look more beautiful in her life. Being pregnant only amplified her loveliness, and the attraction he had for her, the feelings that were in his heart—conflicted as they were—grew crazily in that moment. He was angry with her for being at the house out of duty and pity, and angry at himself for not being able to *stay* angry with her because other feelings always got in the way.

"Are you ready for bed?"

He stared at her. "What?"

She grabbed a pair of pajama bottoms from a pile of

clothes on the chair in the corner and waved them at him. "You can't sleep in sweats."

He looked at the sweats he wore and grimaced at the cut-off leg, realizing that the pj's in her hand had suffered the same fate. "Have you cut up all my pants?"

"Not all of them," she said, and smiled fractionally. "Just a few pairs."

He scowled. "Leave them on the bed."

"Can you undress yourself?"

"I'll be fine."

"Prove it," she said quickly. "Take your sweats off."

Mitch held her gaze steadily, her expression challenging him. "You can leave."

"Uh-uh," she said, and sat on the edge of the bed. "Not until you take them off."

"It's been a while since you've been this eager to get my clothes off," he said, one brow angled. "A month, at least."

He watched as color flushed her neck. After all this time, he could still make her blush.

Calling her bluff, Mitch reached for the drawstring on his sweats. Except that as he moved, pain shot up his back and he grimaced. Tess was at his side in a microsecond, holding the pajamas.

"Let me help."

"I got it," he said, and inched the sweats down over his hips. Except he didn't have it. His ribs hurt so much he could barely lift his shoulders. "Okay, maybe not."

She had his sweats off in about a minute, which was excruciating, since she was close and her hands brushed down his thighs and her touch sent every nerve ending into overdrive. Well, nearly every one. It took every ounce of concentration to stop his body from reacting, busted bones and cracked ribs aside. Her neckline gaped a little, exposing the soft swell of her breasts as she leaned over him, and the look was incredibly sexy.

"Is this when I get my sponge bath?" he asked quietly.

She met his gaze. "Would it put you in a better mood?"

"I think you know exactly what kind of mood it would put me in."

She bit her lower lip and looked at his cast. "Seriously?"

"Do you think I'd let a busted leg stop me?"

She waved the pajamas. "You've never lacked ambition."

He laughed and his ribs ached, but he felt like it was the first time he'd really laughed all week. And damn, it sounded like she was flirting a little.

"Come on," she said, and pulled the pj's over his feet, taking care around the cast. "Do you need a bathroom break?"

"Now that's where I draw the line," he said as he lifted his hips so she could pull the garment up. Her hand brushed over him and he hardened instantly. And damned inconveniently. But he'd never been able to disguise his physical reaction to Tess.

She tugged on her lower lip, ignoring his reaction, finishing the task of pulling up the pants and tying the drawstring. "Now the shirt," she said, and reached for the buttons.

Mitch grasped her hand, linking their fingers intimately. "How much of this do you think I can take?"

"Is that a rhetorical question?"

"It's a you-and-me question," he said. "I don't want to blur the lines."

"The lines between us have always been blurry."

"I guess they have," he agreed.

"I just know I don't want to be at odds with you,

Mitch. I don't want to argue. And I don't want our son to be in the middle." She hesitated, swallowing the obvious emotion in her voice. "When you were in the hospital I was so scared our child would never know you and it made me realize that you were right."

"I was?"

She nodded. "Our son needs us both, fifty-fifty."

"Which means what?"

"That we don't need a lawyer to draw up a custody arrangement," she replied quietly, squeezing his fingers. "We can work out something that's fair to us both, and what's best for our son. Create a routine, you know, so that he doesn't get confused or feel like he's switching between us all the time. I know we can do it if we put his needs first. And that's what I will commit to, Mitch, always putting him first."

"Fifty-fifty," he said, repeating her words. "You in your house, me in mine, and our son with two bedrooms, two sets of toys, two drawers filled with clothes, two lives… Is that how you see it, Tess? Because it looks pretty confusing from here."

"It's the only way." She pulled her hand free.

"From your perspective."

She crossed her arms. "I'm not coming back."

"I know," he said flatly. "But the thing is, you *are* back. For reasons of your own, I know," he added. "You thought I was going to die, and it scared you because the last things we said to one another were filled with hurt and anger. However, you don't get to *be* back, Tess. You don't get to flirt and play nurse and strip off my clothes and bring me trays of food and do all the things a wife would do, because you're *not* my wife. You stopped being my wife the day you bailed on our marriage."

She took a breath. "I know you're upset and—"

"And that's another thing," he said, cutting her off. "Stop pacifying me by suggesting you know how I feel. And stop behaving like you really give a damn, when we both know you're only here out of guilt and obligation. I think I've made it clear I don't need a nursemaid."

Her eyes glittered brightly. "What about a friend?"

Mitch laughed bitterly. "Friends? Is that what we've come to."

"It's something."

He shook his head and reached for her, grasping her hand, entwining their fingers in a way that was excruciatingly intimate. "It's not enough. All or nothing, Tess. And you've made it clear you want to get married one day. Do you think I could stand by and be your *friend* while you married another man? And while someone else gets to be a father to my son when I'm not with him?"

"That's hardly fair, Mitch," she said tightly. "I'm trying to—"

"Clear your conscience," he said, cutting her off again. "I get it. But you can save the guilt trip for someone else. I don't want it. What I want is for you to understand boundaries. And being here in this room, undressing me, touching me, is breaking the rules. Rules you set, I should add, when you made it clear that I had stolen your dreams and your hope four years ago."

As the words left his mouth, Mitch could see the hurt on her face. But he was right to say them. Right to feel them. Right to make it clear that he wanted her to respect the boundaries she'd set. He released her hand, felt the divide between them growing with each passing second.

Instead of capitulating, she glared at him, chest heaving, hands on hips, and then strode from the room and slammed the door. He heard another door slam loudly a few seconds later.

When Jake tapped on the door and came into the room about ten minutes later, Mitch's mood wasn't much improved.

"So, I guess all those banging doors means you and Tess had a fight?" His brother asked as he pulled the curtains shut and sat in the chair by the tallboy.

"Not that it made any difference," he said, frowning. "She won't leave."

Jake grinned. "It's kinda sweet."

"It's nothing of the sort."

"She's always had spirit."

Mitch couldn't disagree. "She drives me crazy."

"That's because you're still in love with her," Jake said, still grinning. "And loves makes a man crazy."

Mitch ignored the accusation. "Even you?"

His brother shrugged. "No comment."

"Abby still lives in town, you know," Mitch remarked and grinned back. Abby Perkins was his brother's high school girlfriend. Who had then turned around and married his best friend when Jake had joined the military. Tom Perkins had died over six years ago, but Abby had remained in town to raise her young son. "She works as head chef at the O'Sullivan hotel. In case you were—"

"I wasn't," Jake said quickly. "Abby and I are ancient history."

"History can repeat itself," Mitch said with irony. "Take it from me."

His brother chuckled. "Which brings me back to the point—you planning on making things right with Tess?"

"Not my decision."

"Have you told her you're still in love with her?" Jake suggested, still grinning. "That might help break the ice."

"Yes," Mitch replied uneasily. "It didn't make any difference."

Jake crossed his arms, sitting back in the chair. "You sure about that? I mean, she's here, isn't she?"

"Guilt," he supplied. "We had an argument the day before the accident. She feels bad about it."

"And how do you feel about it?" Jake asked.

"Tired," he replied. "All we do is hurt one another."

"Not all," Jake reminded him. "You made a baby together."

"You'd think that would be enough, but it's not. You're right," Mitch said irritably. "I love her. I love her so much I can't think straight."

"But?"

"But I'm so damned mad with her for not…for not…"

"Loving you back?" Jake suggested.

"Staying," Mitch amended, and sighed heavily. "She gave up when things got hard."

"Maybe she believed she didn't have any other choice?"

"There's always a choice," he said. "You don't give up on marriage because things become complicated. She wanted me to fall apart when she miscarried that last time, and when I didn't, she punished me by leaving. Now she wants to be friends so we can raise our son in separate houses, and she'll probably marry someone else who I'll end up hating."

Jake sighed and offered a rueful smile. "Maybe you *should* fall apart."

"I can't," he admitted. "I couldn't back then, I can't now. It's not in my DNA."

"Then tell her that," Jake suggested. "At least she'll know how you feel. Better she knows your weakness, rather than thinking you don't feel anything. Maybe she didn't know how to stay and fight for your relationship back then. Maybe leaving was all she left."

Mitch suspected his brother wasn't only talking about

Tess. Jake had his own demons and reasons for leaving Cedar River, most of them to do with Billie-Jack and Abby Perkins.

"I know I should be generous and think that, but I can't," he said, and tapped his chest. "Because despite everything, I know one thing for sure."

"And what's that?" Jake asked.

Mitch took a breath, bracing himself, knowing the words would hurt.

"I would never have left her."

Chapter Eleven

When Tess woke up the following morning it was past eight o'clock. She'd had a restless night, most of it spent staring at the ceiling, magnified by the fact the baby was moving a lot and she couldn't get comfortable in the bed.

She showered and dressed and walked directly past the master bedroom.

The door was closed, anyhow, and she certainly had no intention of entering Mitch's inner sanctum without an invitation. He'd made his thoughts about her presence at the ranch loud and clear. She was intruding, changing the terms of their relationship, making things difficult.

She went into the kitchen to have breakfast and saw the remnants of a tray on the draining board. Mrs. Bailey had obviously been upstairs and had Mitch organized already. Ellie bounded into the kitchen around nine, her usual cheerful self, and showed her a sample of the electronic invitations for the baby shower. Tess was drinking tea and eating toast about ten minutes later when Jake walked in through the mud room.

"Morning," he said as he moved around the counter-top and poured coffee. "Sleep well?"

"Not particularly," she replied, and sipped her tea.

"Any plans for the day?"

"To pack my bag and leave," she replied.

"You know," he said, and looked over the rim of his mug, "there's no need to be hasty."

She raised a brow. "Hasty? You think I should stay?"

"I think it's not my place to tell you or my brother what to do. But," he added, "I'm not sure leaving again would help the situation."

Again? Tess didn't miss the innuendo. "He doesn't want me here."

"I'm not sure he knows what he wants." Jake grinned a little. "You know, could be all the pain meds impairing his judgment. Might be worth giving him the benefit of the doubt. Just saying," he added, and shrugged.

"What do you suggest I do?"

"Nothing," Jake replied. "Just act normal."

"Normal?" she queried, confused. "How do I do that? I'm not even sure what that means for us."

He shrugged again. "I'm not exactly the expert on re-lationships."

"And yet you're full of advice."

"Take it or leave it," he said annoyingly.

"I'm not sure I get your point, Jake."

"I'm pretty sure you do," he said. "You want to make things right, Mitch is being stubborn about it. I guess you still care about him, right?"

She wasn't about to admit to anything. "Does it mat-ter?"

"It might to my brother. It's obvious you're here because you still care about him."

"Well, of course I still care," she said, coloring hotly. "We were married and I'm expecting his child. It's a bond we'll always—"

"You're still in love with him, correct?"

"Well, I—"

"And you won't tell him because that will mean you forgive him for the way he behaved four years ago. Does that about cover it?"

Jake's insight was mortifying. "I can't—"

"Of course you can't," he said, cutting her off as he drained his mug and placed it in the sink. "I get it, you know. I know how it feels to hang onto resentment. But you *should* stick around, Tess."

"Why?" she asked.

He grinned and headed for the door. "Because, like you said, you were married once and now you're having a baby. I know he might act like he wants you to go, but I think we both know that's not the case."

Once he disappeared through the back door, Tess let out a long sigh. *Act normal. Do nothing.* It sounded easy. Not as easy as leaving. But there really wasn't any point to that since she still had to maintain a civil relationship with Mitch because of their baby. Loving him wasn't the point. Raising their child together was all that mattered. She could love him and not be *with* him. Plenty of divorced couples still had feelings for one another. She'd seen the evidence firsthand at parent-teacher discussions over the years. Sometimes divorce was about chronic incompatibility and nothing to do with the depth of feeling. She could be a statistic if it meant her child had two parents who respected one another.

With that in mind, she decided to take his brother's advice and do nothing.

Which was surprisingly easy.

By Wednesday she had her routine down to an art. She prepared his meals, but got Mrs. Bailey to take them upstairs. She let him dress himself, but folded his laundry and left it on the edge of the bed every night while he was asleep. She kept up his pain meds on the bedside table and took daily photos of Chica's foal and sent them to his phone. She met daily with Wes and Ellie to make sure the ranch was running smoothly, and was amazed at how easily she slipped back into life on the Triple C. The next Alvarez foal had been born without complications on Wednesday, and she was delighted to have been able to witness the birth. The colt was strong and healthy, and Alvarez had insisted on first option when the foal was ready for sale.

"So, everything going well?"

Annie's question wasn't unexpected. Her sister had arrived after lunch and they were talking over sodas in the kitchen. "As well as could be expected."

"Are you still hiding out?"

"I'm not hiding," she said. "Simply keeping a low profile."

Annie grinned. "Is it working?"

"We haven't had an argument for days, so that's an improvement."

Her sister chuckled. "Absence makes the heart grow fonder."

"I'm pretty sure all I'm doing is making Mitch madder than hell," she said.

"How long is Jake staying?" Annie asked, one brow up.

Tess shrugged. "That's anyone's guess. Knowing Jake,

he'll ride off on his hog in the middle of the night and then disappear for a few years."

"David thinks he'll hang around until Mitch is back on his feet," Annie mused, and sipped her soda. "Said something about him wanting to reconnect with the family. But, like you said, knowing Jake that doesn't seem likely."

She was about to reply when Ellie came into the room. "Great," the younger woman said to them both. "I have everything arranged for Saturday. The shower will start at one o'clock and go until four. I've had most of the RSVPs back with a yes. Your mom can't make it, but she said to say that she and your dad," Ellie said, and looked toward Annie, "will definitely be here for Thanksgiving. Which is great because I'm planning a big family dinner right here, and this year you can do the turkey because you're a way better cook than me and I know Mrs. B has shown you her secret pear-and-pecan stuffing recipe."

Tess smiled. Ellie's enthusiasm for the holidays was infectious, and she had so many wonderful memories of the festive season from when she had lived at the ranch. "Sounds fabulous."

She stayed in the kitchen with Annie and Ellie for another half an hour, talking about everything from the baby shower to Christmas to more family events that felt bittersweet to Tess. Who knew how Mitch would feel about her coming around for those—if he would even want her around?

Afterward she braced herself and headed upstairs. Mitch was awake and watching television. She remained in the doorway and spoke.

"I just wanted to let you know that Ellie has planned the baby shower here for Saturday."

He looked up and she noticed that he needed a haircut. "I'm not sure why you're telling me," he said, and focused his attention back to the screen. "You seem to do whatever you want around here."

Tess lingered in the doorway, ignoring the fact that he only wore a white tank shirt and a pair of dark cotton boxers. It was warm in the room and the heater was on, which was no doubt why he was half-naked. It took all of Tess's resolve to keep her eyes averted.

"Just keeping you in the loop," she said, and smiled. "Ellie's very excited."

"Delighted to see things are running so smoothly without me."

He still wasn't looking at her. Still looked as mad as thunder.

"The new foals are doing well."

"Yeah," he said flatly. "I got your pictures."

"Do you need anything?"

"To get out of this bed and get my life back."

Tess stepped into the room. He still had over four weeks until the cast came off, although the rest of his injuries were healing well. His eye had improved and she suspected his ribs were also on the mend.

"You seem to be getting around much better."

"Yeah," he said again, staring at the television. "I can get to the bathroom by myself and everything. It's quite an accomplishment."

"I see you've adopted the minimal clothes rule?"

He didn't flinch. "Saves anyone the trouble of having to undress and dress me. Since my nurse appears to be on strike."

"Your nurse was fired," she said, and managed a smile.

He turned his head and met her gaze. "What do you want, Tess?"

"Simply checking in."

"I have enough people checking up on me already. Ellie's here every chance she gets. Jake drops in every hour. Grant says he's taking some time off work so he can stay for a while to keep me company. But I haven't seen *you* for days. If you have something to say, then say it."

"I've been—"

"Slipping into the room unnoticed while I'm asleep and leaving clothes on the end of the bed. I could be blind, deaf and mute and still know you were near me. That's the thing about knowing someone intimately, Tess," he said, his green eyes glittering brilliantly. "It doesn't matter how far apart or how close we are, that connection will always be there."

Her throat ached at his words. "I know."

"How's your belly?"

She stepped forward. "Growing. I have a doctor's appointment at the community hospital tomorrow. You know, to check out the birthing suite there. Annie's coming with me." She added, "I wish you could be there. I'll send you some pictures."

"How long do you plan on staying here?"

"As long as you want me to."

"I don't want you."

Tess was hurt by his quick response, but she wasn't ready to let him off the hook. "I think you do."

"You know what I'm thinking now?"

"I'd like to," she said rawly. "If you'll tell me."

"I tried that already," he said swiftly. "You weren't interested."

"You said you still loved me," she reminded him.

"I know what I said."

Tess looked at him, trying to find something in his expression that indicated he really wanted her to stay.

Because she knew one undeniable fact—*she loved him.*

Still. She'd never stopped. He was the sun to her moon. The air to her lungs. The earth to her feet. And time apart had only amplified that feeling. She was a fool to imagine that love as strong and intense as she'd felt for him would simply fade.

But loving was the easy part.

Forgiving was hard.

Yet, she knew she could. Because, despite what he was saying to her now, they belonged together. With their son. As a family. Mitch had the good sense to see it. Tess realized she'd been living the last few weeks with blinkers on, so wrapped up in resenting him for what had happened in the past that she was blinded from seeing good sense and reason. She did now, and she knew what she wanted. All she had to do was make Mitch see it, too.

"I still love you, too."

He looked away. "Go home, Tess."

There was nothing in his expression that even suggested he was prepared to meet her in the middle. But she wasn't about to concede defeat easily. "You really want me to go?"

He sighed impatiently. "Just to prolong the inevitable? You have your nice little house on Mustang Street, Tess. Surely you want to get back to it?"

"What I want," she said determinedly, "is for you to stop treating me like I'm the enemy."

"I'm not treating you like you're anything," he said. "Just as you wanted."

Tess inhaled and glared at him "Really? Now you're behaving like a spoiled child."

He laughed. "That's the damnable thing about you, Tess. When I wanted you to come back, I was behaving like a controlling jerk. When I said I still loved you, it didn't matter. Now that I want you to go, I'm a spoiled child. There's simply no winning with you, is there?"

She sucked in a sharp breath. *No winning?* Is that what he believed? That she was unbending and had unrealistic expectations? Of him alone? Or of everyone? Had she always been that way? Was she that kind of child? Is that why her mother made sure she had the right shoes and music lessons and a car by her sixteenth birthday? Because her expectations were so high? Was she that wrapped up in herself, that self-absorbed?

Tess stared at the man she loved. Even bedridden and out of action, he was still the most resilient person she had ever known. Even at his weakest, he remained the strongest.

She shuddered. "I want to stay. I love you and I want to be here with you."

"No, you don't. That's just duty talking. Save it," he said. "It's not duty I want, Tess. For the last time, go home."

Tess didn't go home. She stayed. Admittedly, she left him alone. But he heard her. And felt her. And could smell the scent of her fragrance even though she didn't come into the room.

On Saturday, the house was overrun by women. He wasn't invited to the baby shower and didn't want to be. Well, not exactly. But since it was his child they were celebrating, he did experience a feeling of exclusion as he heard the celebrating going on downstairs. There was laughter and glasses clinking and sounds that were clearly about having a whole lot of fun. Grant dropped by and they spent an hour or so talking, and Mitch deliberately avoided mentioning Tess. When his brother left, Mitch grabbed his laptop and did some admin work, trying to take his mind off the party downstairs.

Ellie came upstairs in the afternoon and gave him a plate piled with cake, ignoring his protest about not wanting anything, prattling on about how the day had gone exactly as she'd planned.

"You should see the cute little baseball mitt that Annie gave Tess. And Lucy gave this huge basket of…"

Mitch vaguely listened as his sister spoke, but he was touched that Ellie was so excited about the baby coming. He was excited, too. And he felt guilty he hadn't allowed himself to enjoy that excitement in the last few weeks. His son would be born in a couple of months and he had a whole lot of things he needed to do before then. Get the nursery ready, for one. Work out a schedule for himself, maybe hire a nanny. He knew he would need some help. He didn't doubt that Mrs. B would help, but she had enough to do running the house and feeding the ranch hands every day.

Maybe Winona Sheehan could help, he mused. She'd make a good babysitter for those times he was working. He'd have to run the idea by Tess first. Phase one of their co-parenting plan, he figured. Things seemed calm on that front, at least. She'd sent him pictures from her appointment at the hospital, just a couple of snaps of the room and the amenities. He was grateful for the inclusion and it diluted his resentment a little. Maybe more than a little. He knew they needed to talk, knew they had things to work out, feelings to discuss, but every time they were together all they did was argue.

My fault…

The acknowledgment cut deep. He knew she'd been trying to reconnect, to forge a truce, to make them allies instead of enemies. Mitch also knew he'd been biting her head off nonstop since the accident. But he wasn't going to lay his heart on the line anymore. She'd made her thoughts about the two of them abundantly clear. Still…he didn't enjoy being a mean-spirited jerk. That wasn't his nature. Neither was dwelling on all he'd lost like a lovesick fool. But hearing her say she still loved him was like a stab in his heart. Too little, too late. He didn't want her out of guilt.

It was after four when Tess came upstairs, her arms laden with gifts. She didn't ask if he wanted to see them—she simply laid the items out on the bed and then held up a cute onesie with World's Cutest Kid written on the front.

"Did you have a good day?"

She nodded. "Perfect. It was so good to celebrate the baby with people I care about. Ellie is such a wonderful sister-in-law and—"

"Ex," he reminded her, and flicked through a bath-time book that had pictures of sea animals in it. He determinedly ignored the hurt that flickered across her face.

"How was your day?" she asked.

Mitch waved a hand in an arc. "Living the dream."

"You could have come to the baby shower," she said and smiled. "This is your baby, too."

Unexpectedly she sat on the bed, her pale blue overalls accentuating her middle. She had a sunflower painted on her cheek, and when he looked at it, she smiled.

"Leah did some face painting," she said, and her smile broadened.

Leah, an artist, was David's half sister, born to Sandra and Ivan Petrovic.

"Cute," he said.

"It's about as close to a tattoo as I'll ever get," she said idly, perusing the items on the bed. "You know me, sensible and staid schoolteacher."

The mood between them was lighthearted and one he

wanted to continue. "I always liked that sensible part of you," he said, and dropped the book.

She chuckled. "I thought you would prefer someone with a bit of a wild side."

"Seriously? Why would you think that?"

"Because I'm boring and set in my ways," she replied, and then sighed. "And unforgiving."

She was. But, he suspected, so was he. It was a wall built over years of having to be responsible for everyone and everything. "And your own worst critic," he remarked, reaching out to push back a lock of her hair and tuck it behind her ear. "I've never wanted you to be anything other than who you are."

She met his gaze. "Even though I wanted *you* to be different?"

"Even then."

She sighed, her breath warm against his hand. "And not that I really wanted you to change. Just to be more… more…in the moment."

"Like now?" he asked as he cupped her cheek.

Her eyes widened. "What are you doing?"

"You have cake icing on your lip." He brushed his thumb against her mouth. "I thought I'd remove it for you."

"You told Ellie you didn't want cake," she reminded him.

"I do when it's right here," he said, and leaned a little, ignoring the pain in his ribs, ignoring everything except how soft and welcoming her mouth was beneath his own.

He'd never get enough of tasting her lips, of being with her like this, just the two of them. *Three*, he corrected and gently laid his free hand on her belly. The baby moved and the moment was excruciatingly intimate. Her tongue touched his and she deepened the kiss, moving closer.

Her hand rested gently on his shoulder and was then in his hair. Her touch was like a tonic and he'd been starved of it for too long. She moaned a little, fueling his desire, and Mitch ignored the pain in his chest and the sudden ache in his heart.

"I really," he whispered against her ear, "really want to make love to you right now."

She pulled back a little, biting her bottom lip, threading her fingers through his hair in a way that was torturous. "Really?"

Mitch took a long breath and kissed her cheek. "Really. Only, I'm not sure my busted ribs would be up for it."

She swiveled, propping up on her knees. "We could improvise," she said, and touched his chest, tracing her fingertips down his pectorals, lingering on his rib cage. "If you want."

"If I want," he mused, and curled a hand around her nape, drawing her mouth close. "I want you."

"I should probably lock the door, so we're not interrupted."

It took her about two minutes to pack up all the baby items on the bed, place them on the dresser and lock the door. She returned to the bed, and for the following hour they went on a slow and erotic journey of rediscovery. The last time they'd made love, it had been about heat and sweat and intense physical need and pleasure. This was different. This was about their deep emotional connection, about the years they were together, the years they were apart. The touching, the tasting, the pleasure... None of it would have meant anything if they were strangers or merely casual lovers. Once she was naked she straddled him, taking him deep inside her, her hands linked with his, and she moved...slowly. So slowly it was absolute and aching torture. When he sensed she was near release, he grasped her hips and moved her back and forth in a gentle rhythm. She came apart, moaning his name, sending him over the edge with her.

Afterward she grabbed one of his shirts hanging over the chair and slipped into it, finding a spot on the bed and curling against him.

"Wow," she said softly. "That was something."

"It's always something," he said softly, rubbing her arm.

"I know." She sighed. "So, it seems your ribs are healing okay, after all."

He chuckled. "Well, having you naked and on top of me is quite the motivation to ignore a few cracked ribs."

She gave a sexy groan and curved closer. "Such resilience."

"I don't know if you'd call it that," he teased.

"Just *us*, then," she ventured, and touched his chest. "I was so scared, you know, when you were in hospital. I thought… I thought that our baby might never know his father, and it terrified me."

"You said you needed me."

She gasped and propped up on one elbow. "You heard that?"

"I heard everything. I heard the doctors talking, I heard Ellie crying, I heard Jake come into the room and tell me to stop faking it," he said with a wry grin. "And I heard you. In the end, you were all I heard."

The admission was wrenched from somewhere deep, from the place he never let anyone see. She knew that about him. She knew how tightly wrapped he kept his feelings. Even telling her he loved her for the first time had taken him six months, despite knowing he was utterly in love with her almost from their first date. He didn't make rash decisions. His entire life had been about doing the right thing, staying on the right path, thinking of everyone else first. He knew back then that loving Tess meant changing his life and his family. Taking a risk. He'd had to be sure.

"I'm glad you heard me," she said. "I'm glad it helped you."

"Me, too," he said, and stroked her arm. "I didn't want our son growing up without me, either."

"That's why you didn't give up? Because of the baby?"

"Isn't that why you said our son needed me?" he asked quietly. "To get me thinking? To get me *feeling*?"

"I know you feel things, Mitch," she said, her eyes flashing brightly as she drew circles with her fingers on his chest. "Back then, when we were married, when we were going through...*everything*," she said with emphasis, "I knew you were feeling the same things I was feeling."

"You did? You accused me of being an unfeeling bastard," he reminded her, remembering the time with a heavy heart. "Afraid to feel anything."

She nodded. "I knew you were grieving and unhappy, and I think I was drowning in too much of my own grief to see it at the time. But I know now... I know I was wrong to accuse you of being cold and unfeeling and too afraid to show your emotions."

Mitch stilled. "How do you know now? What's different?"

"Because of this," she said, touching him. "Because we're—"

"Great sex couldn't keep us from breaking apart four years ago. I'm still the same controlling jerk you accused me of being time and time again. I haven't changed, Tess."

"I have," she said softly. "And I know what I want."

"And what's that."

She took a long breath and met his gaze, her eyes glistening. "I want to get married again, Mitch," she said, and smiled. "Please, say you'll marry me?"

Chapter Twelve

"He said no?"

Tess met her sister's incredulous stare. "Yep."

"Um… I thought that marriage was what he wanted?"

"So did I," she replied, still feeling the hurt of his rejection through to her bones. "He said he'd changed his mind and wanted to only share custody of our child. He said that was all that mattered, all he cared about."

"And this was after…" Annie's voice trailed off and she smiled gently. "After you guys, you know."

Tess's skin warmed. "I overestimated what it meant, I guess. You know men and women generally think about sex differently."

It hurt thinking about it. It hurt remembering. After Mitch's quiet dismissal of her suggestion that they get remarried, she'd returned to her own room, packed her bag and left the ranch the following morning without saying goodbye.

That was a week ago and she hadn't heard from him

since other than his daily text asking her if the baby was okay. Nothing about her. Nothing about them.

She knew from Ellie that he was moving around more, spending the days downstairs in the wheelchair and barking out orders to the ranch hands. So it was business as usual at the Triple C. She also knew Jake was still in town. Tess was back in her Mustang Street house, and Joss's daughters still came to see her each afternoon, although Joss made himself scarce.

"What are you going to do?" Annie asked, settling herself on the couch opposite.

"What I planned to do when I first came back to town," she replied. "Have my baby, make some friends, get a job. And stop thinking about Mitch."

Annie offered a gentle smile. "You know, you never did really explain why you changed your mind about the whole marriage thing."

"Mitch nearly died," she said, and stared at her sister. "And I realized I still loved him and I want my child to have both his parents. My son deserves his family. I thought that was what Mitch wanted, too. Epic fail."

"What a jerk."

Tess tried to smile and failed. No matter how much she tried to fake it, the hurt and the rejection stung. He had made his opinion about her idea very clear. He wasn't interested in her proposal. He didn't want a marriage based on duty and guilt. Marrying for the sake of their son wasn't a good enough reason. And he clearly didn't believe she still loved him.

"Are you doing the Thanksgiving thing at the ranch?" Annie asked, and frowned.

Tess shrugged. "I promised Ellie. And since our parents are coming, I need to be there. Frankly, I'd rather be anywhere else than hang out with Mitch at the moment.

But, the baby is only a couple of months away, I really need to get over it. We have birthing classes starting soon and I know he wants to be a part of that."

"I could be your birthing coach?" Annie suggested.

"I know," Tess replied. "But this is something Mitch and I need to do together. By the time the baby comes he'll be out of the cast and back on his feet."

Annie nodded. "If it's any consolation, I'll be there for the holiday to give you moral support."

"Having you close helps," she said to her sister. "I don't know what I'll do when you leave for Colorado."

Annie laughed. "Who says I'm leaving? I haven't decided."

"Is your online love getting cold feet?"

"He's not my anything. We're friends. And besides, the kids wouldn't understand."

"And David?"

"Doesn't see anything other than numbers and stats. I'm not sure he'd even notice if I left."

Tess wasn't so sure. "I think he would."

Annie shrugged loosely. "Maybe. So, I hear you're making the stuffing?"

Tess smiled and they chatted for a while about the upcoming holiday. When her sister left, Tess's cell pinged with a message from Mitch. She replied that the baby was fine. And then nothing.

The following Thursday, Tess headed to the McCall ranch around eleven. Her mother and stepfather had arrived the day before and were staying with Annie. She was so happy to get a hug from her mom that she lingered longer than usual.

As expected, they were concerned when she explained a little about her relationship with Mitch. Her mother knew how much she wanted a child and they were delighted to be becoming grandparents. Determined to keep her parents' concerns at bay, Tess assured them she was happy.

"We're still worried about you," her mother, Suzanne Jamison, said. "Although you do look well. And we're happy you're living close to Annie. How are things with Mitch?"

"Strained," she admitted. "But we're both commited to raising this child together."

"Don't forget you need to find a little happiness for yourself along the way," her mother said.

By they time they arrived at the Triple C, most of the family were already there, except for Hank, who arrived after his shift ended. She met Ellie and Mrs. B in the kitchen and quickly set about making the stuffing for the turkey, doing her best to ignore the sound of Mitch's voice, coming from the front living room where he was hanging out with his brothers. David and Ivan and her stepdad joined the men, while her mom and Annie remained in the kitchen. Ellie was looking at her with a kind of sympathy, and she wondered if Mitch had said something to his sister. She'd never imagined Mitch to be indiscreet, but family was *family* and since she was clearly not going to be a Culhane again, he obviously thought it was okay to tell everyone about her proposal and humiliate her. She could hear them laughing and joking, and every time she registered Mitch's voice, her irritation built. He sounded...*happy*.

How could he be happy when she was miserable?

"Are you okay, Tess?"

She looked at Ellie from across the countertop. "Great. This is fun, don't you think?"

"Um... Tess," Ellie said, and glanced toward Mrs. B. "I told him he was stupid for letting you leave. And Jake said he was chicken," she added, and shrugged. "Can't think of any reason he'd say that, can you?"

Tess's skin heated. "Not one."

Whatever was going on with Mitch, it couldn't possibly have anything to do with her. He didn't want her. He didn't want them. He might love her, but he didn't want her—he wanted his son and that was it.

Because…she'd wounded his pride. The realization hit her with stunning clarity. She'd hurt him. He'd said he loved her and she replied that it didn't matter.

Damn him for being the stubborn one now.

Well, he could stop being stubborn and listen to reason.

"Excuse me," she said as she wiped her hands on a tea towel. "I have to go and talk to Mitch."

The other women all nodded and she left the kitchen. The living room was decorated for the holidays within an inch of its life. Ellie's doing, she figured, noticing there was a vacant space ready for the Christmas tree that would soon go up. Oddly, it filled her with sadness. No, not oddly. She knew why. She'd always loved Christmas at the Triple C. Being at the ranch, finding her own life suddenly integrated back with the Culhanes, only made her yearn for her old life back. For the times when she'd been a part of the family, as much of the glue as Mitch. When they would come to her for counsel and conversation. When she was needed. Loved. And one of them.

All the years in between their divorce and returning to Cedar River, where she'd pretended to be happy, where she'd lived a shadow life, working and existing, had somehow faded amid the reality of being back in the Culhane circle. When the baby came, things would change again. Her son would have a father, and uncles and an aunt and cousins. She'd be a mother. But not a wife.

She saw Mitch by the window, sitting in the wheel-chair, a beer in his hand. Grant and Joss were on the couch, and Jake was on his cell phone by the fireplace. Hank was settled in the seat in the corner chatting to David, and Ivan and her stepdad were talking together. The brothers were all smiling, making jokes and con-versation. And Mitch looked like he wanted to be some-where else. No one else would know, of course. But she knew his expressions; she understood every tilt of his chin, every tightening of his mouth and jaw.

He looked across the room when he realized she was standing in the doorway. The last time they'd seen one another they had made love. And she'd said she wanted to marry him.

And he rejected me...

Like she'd rejected him, over and over again. Out of re-sentment. Out of anger. Out of pride. Out of fear. He'd ac-cused her of wanting to *punish* him for not being who she wanted when they were married, for not grieving with her every time they lost a child, for not understanding how she felt, and then when he threatened to have a vasec-tomy so she wouldn't get pregnant again, she'd reacted.

Overreacted...

Of course it hadn't felt like it at the time. At the time the act of leaving him had felt good. She'd felt vindicated. Avenged. Like she'd won.

In the end, of course, she'd won nothing. Except lone-liness and solitude and heartbreak.

Her hand instinctively came to her belly and his gaze narrowed, watching her. Tess experienced an acute con-nection to him in that moment. Like she had the first time he'd laid a hand on her stomach and felt their baby, and the time they'd shared the joy in watching their child on the ultrasound monitor, or shopping online for baby things, or deciding on a name, discussing schools and their son's future. Things that made them both happy. Because he'd tried. Since she'd returned to town he'd been patient and considerate and made every effort to reconcile their relationship. She was the one who had put a wall up, who'd insisted a reconciliation was impossible. She'd run hot and cold. Wanting him. Needing him. Then blaming and resenting him for that need.

And still, loving him.

"Hey, Tess, how you doing?" Joss said, and tugged at his collar, clearly sensing what he thought was tension between herself and his brother. But Tess knew differently. It wasn't tension. It was awareness. It was memory. It was *them*.

She entered the room and walked around the sofas, coming to a halt in front of Mitch's wheelchair. His eye was healing, and his gaze was as brilliantly green as always. She looked at him, dressed in a blue chambray shirt, a pair of jeans with one leg cut out to accommodate the cast, his broad shoulders so strong and familiar, and a wave of love washed over her.

And she knew what she had to do. And say.

It was time she told the truth.

"I'd like to talk to you," she said quietly.

He met her gaze head on. "So, talk."

Tess glanced around the room for a moment, sensing his brothers, his cousin and her stepfather would like to have the chance to slip from the room. But they didn't. They stayed. A unified front, she thought. Culhanes through to the bone. Always there for each other. Family. The family she wanted to reclaim as her own.

"Can you guys give us a moment?" Mitch asked, glancing around the room.

David and Hank went to move and Tess waved a

hand. "Stay," she said swiftly. If it had to be said in front of his family, so be it. "You were right. The truth is, I blamed you for everything. In a way, I think I blamed you for every baby we lost. I had no reason to do that. No right," she added. "But I did it. I was angry and hurt and so afraid of losing myself, if that makes sense. When you didn't fall apart, too, I resented you...illogically, of course. I thought your silence meant you didn't care, that you didn't *feel*."

"I cared," he said.

Tess nodded. "I know, but when you threatened to have a vasectomy to stop me from getting pregnant again, I believed that was the ultimate betrayal, your way of controlling me and *us*. I didn't think, for one minute, that it might have been your way of staying sane, you know, of coping. That was selfish of me and and I—"

"Tess, I..."

"So, yes, you *were* right. But I think you're so very wrong now," she said, and held up her hand. "I think you're wrong not to give us another chance."

He inhaled sharply. "You said you didn't want—"

"I know what I said," Tess cut in and shuddered, taking a breath, garnering her resolve. "I was angry because I thought you were trying to control me again."

His green eyes glittered. "That's the problem, isn't it Tess? You're always thinking the worst."

The silence in the room was suddenly deafening. She heard one of his brothers clearing his throat, then another. It should have been awkward and uncomfortable, but Tess wasn't hearing or seeing anything other than the man in front of her.

She shrugged, her eyes burning. "Not anymore."

He didn't respond, didn't speak, didn't move. He simply stared at her, his gaze penetrating and impossible to drag her own away from. Tess waited for what felt like an eternity, hoping he'd respond, silently praying he would hold out his hand and draw her close. That he'd forgive her, so they could forgive each other.

But he didn't.

He remained motionless.

The tears in her eyes gathered, plumping at the corners, quickly falling down her cheeks. She glanced around, saw sympathy in his brothers' eyes, in David's eyes, in Ivan's and her stepdad's eyes, as though they knew they probably shouldn't have heard her painful and heartfelt declaration.

"Say something," she whispered.

When the seconds ticked past and he didn't speak, Tess wiped the tears from her cheeks, turned and quickly left the room, hurting through to her core.

Mitch wasn't sure what shocked him more. Tess's words or the fact she'd said them in front of a room full of people. She'd always been an intensely private person—it was one of the things that had drawn them together from the first. Something they had in common. He'd hardly discussed their separation and divorce with anyone, only with David and then, later, with Jake. Mostly because he was so ashamed of the failure. He'd failed his wife and marriage. He'd failed his family by not fighting harder to save what they had.

"Well," Joss said, and shrugged. "That was…interesting."

Jake moved around the room and stood in front of the window, hands on his hips, and shook his head. "You're an idiot."

Mitch was about to scowl and tell his brother to mind

his own business when Hank spoke. "He's right. A complete idiot."

"Yep," Grant agreed. "Totally."

"What the hell do you—"

"Exactly," Jake said impatiently, interrupting him. "A month ago you wanted to reconcile, right?" He hooked a thumb in the direction of the twins. "At least, that's what they said."

"I don't see how it's anyone's business but mine and Tess's," he said flatly, hating that he had somehow found himself under the extreme scrutiny of his four younger brothers, his cousin and dad and Tess's stepfather, *and* the fact that were all regarding him as though he had lost his mind.

"That's the thing about this family," Jake reminded him. "We get to know everyone's business, whether we like it or not. A precedent, I would like to add, that you set. So, if you want to dish out advice, like you are known to do, be prepared to take it."

Mitch stilled instantly. "Is that what I do?"

"Always," Joss said. "Damn annoying at times. But we're used to your high road. Did you really threaten to have a vasectomy so Tess wouldn't get pregnant again?"

He shrugged. "It was a tough time."

"That's why she left?" Grant asked, frowning deeply. "She wanted a baby and you said you wouldn't give her one? I always thought *you'd* screwed up, but I didn't imagine it was by doing something so damned selfish. Not surprising she walked out."

Mitch stared at his brother and guilt pressed down on his shoulders. And shame. Because his brother was right. He had been selfish. *My wife wanted a child. I said no.* And suddenly, as hard as he tried, Mitch couldn't articulate one good reason other than the obvious for being so pigheaded all those years ago. Because he *was* selfish. And used to getting his own way. According to his rationale, she'd behaved unreasonably and hadn't believed their marriage was enough to make them happy. Her wanting a child, after losing so many, had been like a slap in the face to everything they *did* have. That's why he'd said he would have a vasectomy—to make her see sense. To get his own way. *To be in control.*

And when she returned to Cedar River, pregnant with his child, he wanted to be in control again. Her refusal to get married was another slap in the face, another reminder that they'd lost everything they'd once had. And another reminder of his failure as a husband, a father, protector and as a man.

It hurt. A lot.

So did her sudden turnaround after the accident. Because he didn't want her out of guilt or pity or duty. Except, she'd said she loved him. And he was scared to believe her because he loved her with such aching intensity that the thought of losing her again scared him through to his bones.

He stared at Jake. "I do love her."

"Yes," Jake said quickly. "We all know that. You're the best man I know, Mitch, and we all admire you for everything you've done for us over the years. But if you let Tess walk out of your life, then what the hell is wrong with you?"

Mitch looked at his brothers, listening to them all as in turn they voiced their opinions about his behavior toward Tess, and about his controlling ways, and how much he believed he knew everything about everyone and had unrealistic expectations of those he loved. He looked at Tess's stepdad and saw the older man's disappointment.

He saw his best friend, David, looking as though he knew exactly what he was thinking.

Right. So, he was an overbearing and impossible to please.

And he laughed. Loudly. Once he'd finished laughing, his brothers and the others were all watching him incredulously. And clearly waiting for his next move.

"And now that you've all finished playing Cupid *and* judge and jury," he said, and placed his hands on the chair wheels, "if you'll excuse me, I think I need to go and apologize."

Jake was grinning. "Hallelujah. Go fix it."

When Mitch wheeled into the kitchen, he saw Mrs. B behind the counter, Ellie cutting up pumpkin, Annie decorating a cake and Tess's mother clipping beans. Tess was by the table, mixing something in a bowl. She looked so damned beautiful she took his breath away. She wore a blue denim dress, dark tights and a pale cardigan. Her hair was up in a clip and her bangs fell across her forehead. Her belly was rounded and an intense sense of love washed over him. He'd never, in all his life, tire of looking at her. He cleared his throat and they all looked toward the doorway.

"Ladies," he said quietly, meeting Tess's gaze head-on. "If you don't mind, I'd like to talk to my wife privately."

No one blinked an eye at how he'd referred to her as his wife. Except for Tess. One of her brows arched steeply and her mouth pressed into a tight line. She stopped what she was doing and dropped the spoon into the bowl. Mrs. B hurriedly ushered Ellie from the room, Annie and Tess's mom quickly followed, and within seconds they were alone.

Looking tired, she eyed him. "What do you want now?"

Mitch wheeled in a little farther, mindful not to whack

his cast on the table, swallowing hard. "All those years ago... I did fall apart. I just never let you see it. Scared, I guess," he admitted hoarsely. "Of you somehow thinking I was weak and foolish because I'd failed you."

She looked at him. "I would never have thought that."

"*I* did," he said, and tapped his chest. "In here. It was my job to protect you, to keep you safe, to keep you from hurting. And I couldn't," he said, his insides aching. "I knew you were heartbroken and grieving, and logically I knew you wanted me to feel that, too. And I did feel it, Tess. I felt it every time I looked at you, every time I saw your tears and your unhappiness. But I was helpless. I couldn't make things right. I couldn't tell you it would work out...because I had no idea if it would. And that lack of control was unimaginable to me." He sucked in a breath, perhaps the heaviest of his life. "Since my mom died and, hell, maybe even before then, I had to step up and look after things around here. Billie-Jack was never much of a father, even when he was sober. Mom kept everything together, you know, she made things work. When she died I had to step into those shoes, and even more so after Billie-Jack left. And I guess, along the way, I stopped being me and became mom and dad and anything else everyone needed. So, I'm sorry," he said, and realized his hands were shaking. "I'm sorry I failed you. And hurt you," he added softly. "Because hurting you is the last thing I would ever want to do."

"I guess we hurt each other in different ways," she said quietly, not moving.

He inhaled and sighed. "I didn't think of what that would mean to you, to take away our ability to have a baby together, even though I thought I knew how much you wanted a child. I didn't consider your feelings. All I did was think about how it would fix things. I had a problem. That was the solution. Stupid," he said, running a weary hand through his hair. "And arrogant. And typical of me, I guess. When you left I became so wrapped up in righteousness, I didn't see that arrogance. Maybe I didn't want to see it. I was angry because I'd convinced myself you didn't think we were enough. Like, if there was only you and me, and no kids, then that wasn't enough for you. We weren't enough. *I* wasn't enough."

"I never thought that."

He nodded and then shrugged. "Maybe if we'd talked more. If *I'd* talked more," he corrected. "I know you tried. I know I closed down and it probably seemed as though I was shutting you out. The truth is," he admitted as emotion closed his throat, "I was broken and didn't know how to fix myself. Every time we lost a child, I really *did* want to cry with you, Tess... I just didn't know how."

"Well, we're talking now," she said, and crossed her arms. "That's something."

"It's not enough." He inched closer. "Will you sit down?" he asked, and motioned to the dining chair beside him. "Please."

She took a long breath and then slowly moved around the table, perching on the edge of the chair. "Okay, I'm sitting."

Mitch grasped one of her hands and entwined it with his. "The thing is, as much as it might seem to the contrary, I love you, Tess, more than anything or anyone."

"Are you sure?" she asked.

"Positive. And I want to marry you, if you'll have me."

She tightened her fingers around his. "You didn't want to marry me last week after we...you know...after..."

Mitch stroked her palm with his thumb and laid his other hand on her belly. "Pride. Ego. Control." He grinned a fraction. "You know, all those things you love about me that sometimes make me act like a total jerk."

She scowled. "I don't think—"

"Exactly." He brought her hand to his mouth, gently kissing her knuckles. "Stop thinking. I reckon that's been part of our problem—we both *overthink* everything. From now on, let's simply feel, okay?"

"I'm sure you're too much of a control freak to do that."

He shrugged. "You're probably right. And it'll take some work, and no doubt you'll have to keep me in line… but, sweetheart, you know as well I do that we're worth it."

She looked suspicious. "What are you saying?"

Mitch smiled. "I'm saying that I am devotedly in love with you. I'm saying that you are the only woman I have ever loved. The only woman I *will* ever love. I'm saying that I want to marry you. I want to be your husband again. I want to love you and protect you and be beside you, always. If you'll have me."

"I already said I wanted to get married again," she reminded him, her expression softening a fraction. "And you said no, remember?"

"Haven't we already covered the part where I admitted I was a stupid jerk last week?" He chuckled. "Look, after the accident, I thought you were hovering around me because you felt guilty that I almost died. I know," he said, and held up a hand when he saw her sharpening expression. "Out of line. Not one of my better qualities."

"Of course I felt guilty." She sighed. "I said some terrible and hurtful things to you…things I wanted to take back. But I never stopped loving you. Not ever."

Mitch's heart rolled over. "Will you marry me?"

She nodded, her eyes glistening. "Of course I will.

And since I'm an old-fashioned kind of girl, can we do it before the baby arrives?"

"We'll do it as soon as possible," he replied.

She shuddered. "And can you forgive me for every terrible thing I've said to you?" She asked the question quietly. "Not only these past few weeks, but from the beginning?"

"Only if you forgive me in return. The thing is, Tess, I think we hurt the person we love the most because we know that person will always have forgiveness in their heart. I love you," he saw rawly and touched her rounded stomach, feeling their baby, loving them both more in that moment than he imagined he could ever love anyone. "I'd give my life for you and our son."

"I know you would," she said, and leaned in, kissing him softly on the mouth. "Part of the reason I love you so much is how you protect the people you care about. Even during those times you don't think you're doing such a great job. Your strength of character is amazing. And I want to be your wife again. I want to live here and help you run this place and be by your side for the rest of my life."

Mitch curled a hand around her nape. "Me, too," he said, and grabbed her left hand. "I better get a ring."

She smiled. "I still have my old rings."

He thought about it for a moment and then shook his head. "How about we buy new rings, for our new start?"

She nodded. "I like that idea."

"And," he said, and kissed her softly, lingering along her jaw, "I guess we should head back into the living room to tell the gang we're back together before they come looking for us."

"Too late!"

Ellie's cheerful voice echoed from the doorway and

within seconds the entire clan piled into the room, including Mrs. B. It wasn't long before her parents and then Annie and David arrived in the room, and his kids and father in tow. Suddenly the kitchen was crammed with Culhanes and McCalls and her parents. They were congratulated and they were hugged. Grant pulled some champagne from the refrigerator and they shared a toast. Everyone he loved was in the room, Mitch thought as he sat beside Tess, their hands entwined.

"Let's get this Thanksgiving feast started," Joss said, and patted his stomach. "I'm starving."

Tess leaned in close. "I guess we do have a lot to be thankful for this year," she whispered.

Mitch touched her cheek. "That we do."

He looked around, hearing his brothers dissing one another. Ellie was frowning at something Grant said about her upcoming midterm exams. Mrs. B was humming as she cooked. David's kids and Joss's girls were racing back and forth in a game of tag, and her parents were sitting together and watching them approvingly, and Tess looked insanely beautiful and peaceful.

Yep. He felt like the luckiest man on the planet. Mitch smiled, happier than he had ever been in his life.

Epilogue

"I don't know why you're panicking," Tess said calmly as they headed for the hospital.

"I'm not panicking," Mitch assured her, although she knew her husband's adrenaline was clearly running into overdrive. "I just wasn't expecting to become a father on Christmas Day."

Tess smiled and maneuvered her belly behind the seat belt. "It's just a little over a week earlier than expected. And I spoke to Lucy and she said not to worry. Dr. O'Sullivan is on duty and will be there for the delivery."

Mitch glanced sideways. "You're so calm."

"I've been waiting for this moment for a long time," she said softly, and grabbed his hand.

"Me, too." He sighed. "We should have called the ambulance."

"My water hasn't broken yet," she reminded him. "There's still time between the contractions. Stop worrying."

"Feels like my middle name at the moment."

She smiled gently. "You do realize that most of your family are following us right now."

He glanced in the rear-vision mirror and at the headlights. "It's a big deal."

"I know," she said, well aware that his brothers and sister were looking forward to welcoming their son into the family fold. One thing their child would never lack, she knew, was love.

They arrived at the hospital at ten o'clock that evening and Tess was immediately ushered into the birthing suite. Mitch was a bundle of nerves, but she was oddly calm, and so looking forward to meeting their son. She was immensely grateful for having a relatively trouble free pregnancy, considering her history. Strangely, carrying this child had felt different from her previous pregnancies. She couldn't explain it, but even in those early months, she'd always known she would carry her child to term and have a healthy baby.

The doctor came to see her soon after she was settled and once her water broke around midnight, their son arrived several hours later, screaming and perfect and with a head of dark hair just like his father.

Who, she discovered, was an amazing birth coach and helped her through every moment. Through every pain she experienced, every time she cried, through her exhaustion and finally her joy as their son was laid against her breast.

Charlie Alexander Culhane arrived at three fifteen on Christmas morning and weighed a hefty eight pounds three ounces. He was perfect, and she couldn't stop staring at him in wonder for the next hour.

Mitch was at her side, smoothing back her hair. "He's incredible."

She looked up, spotted tears plumping at the corners of his eyes and smiled gently. "I know. Thank you."

He smiled and his beautiful green eyes glittered, filling with tears. It was the first time in ten years she'd witnessed him show such intense emotion without any walls up. "You did all the work."

"It was a team effort."

He touched their son's tiny head. "I have no real words for what I'm feeling right now. It's all sort of surreal."

His admission was heartfelt and raw, and seeing him so vulnerable made her throat ache. They'd come a long way, taking the longest road to get to where they now were. But every bump, every diversion, was worth it when she considered all she now had. They'd married a couple of weeks after Thanksgiving, choosing to have a simple ceremony at the ranch, surrounded by their family and a few friends and performed by the same celebrant who had married them the first time. That was followed by a quiet buffet lunch and then they headed into town and spent their wedding night in a luxurious room at the O'Sullivan Hotel. Mitch was getting around on crutches by then, and thankfully was able to stand by her side during the ceremony.

And, now, they had their son.

"I love you." She touched his cheek, drawing away the tears with her thumb. "So very much."

"I love you, too, Tess," he said, his voice raw. "And I'm so happy we didn't give up on each other."

They never would, she thought, cradling their son, looking at the man who was her best friend, her lover, her husband, and she realized she really had gotten her happily-ever-after.

* * * * *

Don't miss Jake's story,
the next book in
Helen Lacey's new miniseries,
The Culhanes of Cedar River,
Available December 2019,
wherever Harlequin books
and ebooks are sold.

SPECIAL EXCERPT FROM

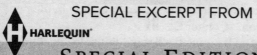

HARLEQUIN®

SPECIAL EDITION

*Alyssa Santangelo has no memory of the
past seven years—including her divorce—but she
remembers her love for Connor Bravo. One way
or another, she's going to get her husband back.*

Read on for a sneak preview of
A Husband She Couldn't Forget,
the next book in Christine Rimmer's
The Bravos of Valentine Bay *miniseries.*

An accident. I've been in an accident. The stitches they'd
put in her knee throbbed dully, her cheeks and forehead
burned and she had a mild headache. Every time she took
a breath, she remembered that the seat belt had not been
very nice to her.

She must have made a noise, because as she sagged
back to the pillow again, Dante flinched and opened
his eyes. "Hey, little sis." He'd always called her that,
even though she was second eldest, after him. "How you
feelin'?"

"Everything aches," she grumbled. "But I'll live."
Longing flooded her for the comfort of her husband's
strong arms. She needed him near. He would soothe all
her pains and ease her weird, formless fears. "Where's
Connor gotten off to?"

HSEEXP0919

Dante's mouth fell half-open, as though in bafflement at her question. "Connor?"

He looked so befuddled, she couldn't help chuckling a little, even though laughing made her chest and ribs hurt. "Yeah. Connor. You know, that guy I married nine years ago—my husband, your brother-in-law?"

Dante sat up. He also continued to gape at her like she was a few screwdrivers short of a full tool kit. "Uh, what's going on? You think you're funny?"

"Funny? Because I want my husband?" She bounced back up to a sitting position. "What exactly is happening here? I mean it, Dante. Be straight with me. Where's Connor?"

Don't miss
A Husband She Couldn't Forget
by Christine Rimmer,
available October 2019 wherever
Harlequin® Special Edition books and ebooks are sold.

www.Harlequin.com

Looking for more satisfying love stories
with community and family at their core?

Check out **Harlequin® Special Edition**
and **Love Inspired®** books!

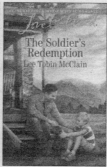

New books available every month!

CONNECT WITH US AT:

Facebook.com/groups/HarlequinConnection

 Facebook.com/HarlequinBooks

 Twitter.com/HarlequinBooks

 Instagram.com/HarlequinBooks

 Pinterest.com/HarlequinBooks

ReaderService.com

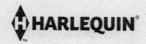

**ROMANCE WHEN
YOU NEED IT**

HFGENRE2018

Love Harlequin romance?

DISCOVER.

Be the first to find out about promotions, news and exclusive content!

Facebook.com/HarlequinBooks

Twitter.com/HarlequinBooks

Instagram.com/HarlequinBooks

Pinterest.com/HarlequinBooks

ReaderService.com

EXPLORE.

Sign up for the Harlequin e-newsletter and download a free book from any series at **TryHarlequin.com.**

CONNECT.

Join our Harlequin community to share your thoughts and connect with other romance readers!
Facebook.com/groups/HarlequinConnection

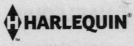

HARLEQUIN®

**ROMANCE WHEN
YOU NEED IT**